THE ROGUE WAVE

THE ROGUE WAR

THE ROGUE WAVE

A Novel

PAUL NICHOLAS MASON

CANADA

*Publisher's note: This book is a work of fiction. Names, characters, places and
incidents are either the product of the author's imagination or are used
fictitiously, and any resemblance to actual persons living or dead
is entirely coincidental.*

Library and Archives Canada Cataloguing in Publication

Title: The rogue wave : a novel / Paul Nicholas Mason.

Names: Mason, Paul Nicholas, author.

Identifiers: Canadiana 20200384244 | ISBN 9781989689219 (softcover)

Classification: LCC PS8576.A85955 R64 2021 | DDC C813/.54—dc23

Printed and bound in Canada on 100% recycled paper.

Now Or Never Publishing
901, 163 Street
Surrey, British Columbia
Canada V4A 9T8

nonpublishing.com
Fighting Words.

We gratefully acknowledge the support of the Canada Council for the Arts
and the British Columbia Arts Council for our publishing program.

To Nathalie,
My Beloved Wife

CHAPTER ONE

When you drown, you drown. It's simple. You were alive, and then you're dead.

Matthew Harding's detective agency advertised an unlikely specialty—"Cases with a metaphysical dimension." It could scarcely have been otherwise, as Matthew was *obsessed* with metaphysical questions. He wrestled with whether God exists, how the universe came to be, and what accounts for the presence of evil in the world, with the same focus that other men bring to sports teams, or cars, or porn stars. His home was filled with religious statuary, his recreational travel focused on sacred sites. The second bedroom in his condo had over eight hundred books devoted to religious studies.

A legacy, carefully invested, from his generous Aunt Hilda, kept him solvent and his agency doors open, even when no clients crossed the threshold for months at a time, leaving his beautiful secretary Sharon hundreds of hours to work on a degree in English literature online—while occasionally cruising gossip sites or posting pictures of her cockapoo to Instagram. Matthew, meanwhile, sat moodily at his desk, reading Tolstoy, Dostoevsky, and Bulgakov, recognizing that the Russians wrestled with the same questions that agitated his own soul. Every now and then, however, he ventured out to have tea with his psychologist friend Dr. Barker, the two of them sharing a table at Sandy's Coffee and Muffins shop a few doors away from their own offices on Prospect Avenue in Toronto.

On a hot and humid Thursday afternoon in late July a man in his early thirties stepped through the office door of Harding's Investigations and presented himself at Sharon's desk.

"How may I help you?" asked Sharon, brushing aside a strand of dark hair from her face, and not bothering to minimize TMZ—the gossip website she was visiting.

"I'd like to see the detective, please," said the man. Most men might have taken a moment to savour Sharon's beauty, but this one was distraught.

"Is he expecting you?" Sharon asked. She knew he wasn't, but there was a protocol to be observed, even in an office as quiet as Harding's Investigations.

"No," said the man. "I didn't call ahead. I saw the sign outside and came in."

"I'll see if he's busy." Sharon picked up her phone. "There's a gentleman wishing to see you," she said. "Are you free?"

"I'm free," replied Matthew with a tone of distracted surprise. He rose to greet his guest as Sharon ushered him in.

"My name is Andrew Greenfield," said the guest as the two men shook hands. "I think I need your services, but I don't know. I've never hired a detective before."

"Please," said Matthew, indicating the empty chair. "Tell me what your problem is, and I'll tell you whether I can help."

Andrew seated himself and gripped the arms, as if desperate to have something to hang onto. "My girlfriend has disappeared," he said. "Hannah. Hannah Hutchinson. We were out in New Brunswick, on a whale-watching boat. We were hit by a big wave. A *rogue* wave, they said. She was swept overboard."

"I'm so sorry," said Matthew. "I remember the news coverage. This was a couple of months back?"

"Yes," said Andrew. "June 4th. We were on holiday. Our first trip together."

"As I recall," said Matthew, "she was the only one whose body wasn't recovered."

"Yes." Andrew flinched, closed his eyes. "Six drowned, thirty-eight survivors picked up by other boats. The Coast Guard searched for hours."

"I see." Matthew paused a moment. "It's a tragic case, but isn't it relatively straightforward? A rogue wave—a number of drownings. I don't want to waste your money, Mr. Greenfield."

Andrew locked eyes with Matthew. "Two days ago, I got an email from a friend in Edmonton," he said. "He'd sent me a video on YouTube. It's a wedding in Huajuapan, Mexico. Hannah is in the video." He pushed his phone across the desk.

Matthew pressed play. The video lasted a little over fifty seconds. It was a single shot panning from the bride, groom, and celebrant over the bridesmaids to the congregation. The setting appeared to be a large hall. The people seated were mostly native Mexicans, but the camera lingered briefly on a small, blonde, white woman sitting beside a short-haired man of indeterminate race. She looked uncomfortable—even, perhaps, traumatized.

"The small blonde woman?" said Matthew.

Andrew nodded. "Hannah. My girlfriend. My fiancée."

"And do you recognize the man she's sitting beside?"

"I've never seen him before."

"Okay. Okay." Matthew chewed on his bottom lip. "Is it possible that the video was taken some time ago but only posted recently?"

"No," said Andrew. "Hannah had never visited Mexico—and she's wearing the brooch I bought her in New Brunswick."

"I see." Matthew fast-forwarded to the woman, and paused the video. "She doesn't look happy."

"She looks scared," said Andrew. "Really scared." He choked up. Matthew handed him a box of tissues.

"I would like to help," said Matthew, "but I need to warn you this could get expensive. I should visit both New Brunswick and Huajuapan—those places at least—so there's the matter of my travel and accommodation expenses. Are you able . . . ?"

"I can write you a cheque for $10,000 right now," said Andrew. "We had a wedding account. Will that cover things?"

"I don't charge for my time unless I'm successful," said Matthew, "so that will cover expenses for a few weeks. Now, may I ask you to send me the link, and any photos you have of Hannah? Here's my email address." He handed Andrew his card and Andrew put a cheque on the desk. "And I'll also need to see anything else you may have of hers. Documents. Letters. Telephone numbers for her family."

"I'm sending everything I have on my phone right now," said Andrew. "Anything else I can collect at home and put in a package for you. Shall I bring it back tomorrow morning?"

"Why don't I come for it tonight?" said Matthew. "I anticipate flying out to New Brunswick early tomorrow morning." And so it was agreed. The two men shook hands again, and Andrew left, muttering a *thank you* to Sharon on his way out.

Sharon got up and tapped her fingers on Matthew's office door. "Do we have a case, Matt?" she asked.

"We have," said Matthew, glancing up from his computer. "Let me show you something." Sharon joined him behind the desk, and Matthew indicated a photograph of Andrew and a small blonde woman, both smiling into the camera. "Our client, and his fiancée, Hannah." He closed the picture, then clicked on the video, fast-forwarded, and froze on a good image of the woman. "Same person?" he asked, looking up at Sharon. "Your eyes are sharper than mine."

"Yes," said Sharon, without hesitating. "Pretty girl."

"She's missing," said Matthew. "Believed to have drowned courtesy of that rogue wave in New Brunswick two months ago. This video was taken some time between then and now. In Mexico."

"She looks like she's seen a ghost," said Sharon.

"Well, arguably that beats *being* a ghost," said Matthew. "At any rate, something's very wrong. Can you please book me a flight to Saint John tomorrow morning?"

"Sure," said Sharon. "Return?'

"No, said Matthew. "I'll be flying on to Mexico, but I'll book that one myself. I don't know how long I'll be in New Brunswick."

"It's good to be working again," said Sharon. "It's been nearly two months."

"This is a strange one," said Matthew. "I'm not sure where it will take me."

CHAPTER TWO

Matthew did not leave for home immediately. Packing his travel case would only take ten minutes, and he needed to give Andrew time to gather the items he had asked for. He left his office and walked west on Prospect to the office of his psychologist friend, Dr. Barker. There, he greeted Marika, the receptionist, a striking young black woman in an elegant yellow dress.

"Is Jordan with a patient?" he asked.

"Another five minutes, Matthew," said Marika, "then he'll want to make some notes. Are you going to Sandy's?"

"Yes," said Matthew. "If he isn't seeing someone else immediately, I'd be glad of his company."

"I'll tell him," said Marika, smiling. "And please tell him to bring me a bran muffin."

"I'll buy you one and send it back with him," said Matthew, giving her a little wave on his way out.

Sandy's Coffee & Muffins shop was in the same block as Matthew's and Jordan's offices. It was small, a bit dingy, and the menu was stunningly sparse—coffee, tea, milk, bran muffins, cinnamon toast, grilled cheese sandwiches and, if Sandy were feeling ambitious, soup. Sandy himself was a little elf of a man in his early forties, and the shop's only employee, but the location was a good one as there were no Tim Hortons or Starbucks for at least three blocks.

"Tea for here, and two bran muffins to go," said Matthew, nodding to Sandy. "In separate bags."

"Jordan joining you?" asked Sandy.

"Yes, but not for another ten minutes."

Sandy plugged in the kettle. There were two other customers in the store: an older man buried in a newspaper, and a smartly dressed, middle-aged woman nursing a coffee.

"Hello, Jane," said Matthew to the woman.

"My favourite private eye," said Jane. "You hot on the trail of someone?"

"Not right at this moment," said Matthew. "How's work for you?"

"Thank God for kinky men," said Jane, bringing her palms together as if in prayer.

"I'm sure they're grateful for your services," said Matthew politely. He sat down a couple of tables away and took a small, slim book out of his shirt pocket—a copy of the *Tao Te Ching* in tiny print. Opening it randomly he read:

> *Intelligence comes from knowing others,*
> *But to know oneself brings wisdom.*
> *There is strength in mastering others*
> *But true power comes from mastering oneself.*
>
> *You are rich when you recognize that you have enough.*
> *When you accept the inevitability of death,*
> *You achieve immortality.*

Is this wisdom? he asked himself—not for the first time. *Or is this an ancient equivalent of a Hallmark greeting card?* When reading the *Tao* he was never quite sure, but he kept returning to it. When he read the Sermon on the Mount, he felt that he was engaging with something radical, even revolutionary, but his response to the *Tao* was more complicated, ambivalent. Would his understanding of the text be fundamentally different if he understood classical Chinese? But then not knowing Koine Greek had not frustrated his engagement with the gospels. In any event, he realized he would have very little time for reading the *Tao*, or anything else, in the next little while.

"Whatcha reading, Matthew?" asked Jane. She slid her finger along the spoon lying in front of her, dipping the tip into the trace of coffee in the small shallow bowl.

"The *Tao*," said Matthew. "The *Tao Te Ching*. It's a Taoist text—an ancient scripture."

"I know what the *Tao* is," said Jane. "Every dominatrix has a copy." She laughed. "No, I studied it at Queen's. Third year World Religions course."

"I didn't know you studied religion," said Matthew.

"It was an elective," said Jane. "My major was Women's Studies." She licked the coffee off her fingertip.

Sandy arrived at Matthew's table with a pot of tea and a mug. "Mine was Sociology," he said. "Ask me anything you like about Foucault or Lacan. And I sling coffee and bran muffins for a living."

"I don't have a degree," said Matthew. "I'm just a community college boy."

"Hey, we all follow our own bliss," said Jane. "Hello, Doctor."

Jordan Barker had quietly entered the shop. "Hello, Jane," he said. "Matt. Sandy." He was a short man, lean, and dressed in a tailored suit.

"Coffee, Doc?" said Sandy. "And I haven't forgotten your muffins, Matthew." He went back behind the counter.

"This girl's bed is calling her," said Jane, rising to her feet. "Have a good afternoon, gentlemen."

"Take care of yourself," said Matthew.

"Always," said Jane. She picked up her briefcase and headed for the door, leaving a five-dollar bill by the cash register.

"So," Jordan said. "A muggy day."

"It is," Matthew said. And then: "I have a strange case." He gave Jordan some of the details, without mentioning his client's name. His friend listened, breaking eye contact only to acknowledge the arrival of his coffee.

"It *is* a strange case," Jordan said. "Who will you speak to in New Brunswick?"

"The captain of the whaling boat, I hope," said Matthew. "And whoever the RCMP assigned to the case."

"Do you have any suspicions?" asked Jordan.

"I don't know what to think yet," said Matthew. "There *was* a wave—a rogue wave. People died. Could she have been swept overboard and picked up by some passing boat? Surely, they would have delivered her to the authorities, in that case—in Canada or maybe the US. The weird detail is Mexico. It's a long way from New Brunswick."

"Unless she wanted to get away," said Jordan.

"My client doesn't strike me as the kind of man a woman would want to escape," said Matthew. "But it's early days yet. I'll need to talk to her friends, her parents."

Sandy brought the muffins to the table. Matthew pushed one toward Jordan. "For Marika," he said. "You're starving that poor woman."

Jordan laughed. "Good luck with the case," he said, as Matthew fished out his wallet. "And enjoy New Brunswick."

Chapter Three

Prospect Avenue was busy at 3:20: the afternoon crush was building, and there was a steady flow of traffic. Matthew was halfway to his office when he saw an unkempt man improbably dressed in a winter coat heading towards him. His wild hair and sun-darkened face made it difficult to guess his age, and he was talking to himself and gesticulating wildly. "I'm talking to you, I'm talking to you, I'm talking to you," he said. "Listen. *Just listen—*"

At that instant, a late model GM car veered off the road. It bounced over the curb, missing Matthew by several feet, but crashed into the wild man, propelling his torso over the hood and squashing his pelvis and legs between the bumper and the front of a store selling marijuana paraphernalia. The man made no sound, and Matthew guessed that the impact had killed him, or, at least, shattered his spine. He whipped out his cell phone and dialed 911. A woman down the street screamed—once, twice. People spilled out of storefronts on both sides of the avenue.

"There's been an accident at 346 Prospect," Matthew said to the dispatcher. "One man seriously injured . . . Matthew Harding. I'll stay here."

He stepped around the car, hoping that he might be able to do something for the victim. As he did, the driver's side door opened and a broad-shouldered young man jumped out and ran from the accident. He crashed into a couple of other people on the sidewalk, shoving them aside. Marika, who had just come out onto the pavement herself, tried to stop him, but he knocked her off her feet. Sharon came out onto the street an instant after he passed Harding's Investigations. She ran to join Matthew, who had, in the meantime, jumped into the car and turned off the engine, causing it to back up just a little, thus taking a bit of pressure off the man pinned between it and the storefront.

Sharon gently took the victim's hand. "Can you hear me?" she asked. There was no response.

Matthew joined her. "I've called for an ambulance," he said. "Christ, the poor bastard." There was blood coming out of the man's mouth and pooling on the hood.

An older woman joined them. "The poor man," she said. "Do you know him?"

"No," said Matthew.

"Was the car aiming at him?" asked Sharon. She glared at a young woman taking a video just a few yards away.

"I don't know," said Matthew. "It doesn't seem likely, but it was accelerating. . . . Hold on, sir—help is coming." There was no response, but an instant later everyone heard a siren, and then another, approaching from different directions. "Thank God," said Matthew.

Paramedics went to work on the victim—though there were no signs of life—and the police established a cordon, ushering onlookers behind yellow tape on both sides of the accident.

"You Harding?" a policeman asked Matthew. "Speak to you over here, please?" Matthew gave a quick description of the events.

"You say the driver ran away, sir?" said the officer.

"He did. About a minute after impact."

"Could you describe him?"

Matthew paused for a moment. "Male, mostly Caucasian, between twenty-eight and thirty-four, broad-shouldered, wearing a red, button-up, short-sleeved shirt, blue jeans, Converse running shoes." He took a breath. "Short dark hair, no beard or mustache. Small ears. Big nose."

The officer looked surprised. "That's an unusually detailed description," he said.

"I notice things," Matthew replied.

The policeman nodded. "Anything else you remember?"

Matthew thought hard. He could see his friend Jordan about twenty feet away, and noted the concern etched on his face. "I think I need to repeat that the car accelerated as it hit the curb," he said. "I don't know if his foot hit the gas by mistake—but he wasn't braking. And his head was up. He was looking straight ahead when he made contact."

"Okay," said the officer. "And your office is a few doors down?"

"Right there," said Matthew, gesturing with his head.

"Will you be in the city for the next few days?"

"No," said Matthew, "I'm flying out to New Brunswick tomorrow morning, but I'll be in touch with my secretary every day. And I answer calls and text messages quickly. You have my card."

The officer nodded. "I suspect someone will be in touch," he said. "Thank you for your assistance." He closed his notebook. "Are you all right, sir?"

"I'm a little shaken up, to be honest," said Matthew. "But I'm in much better shape than that poor fellow." They looked at the victim, who was being carried on a spinal board toward the ambulance.

"Would you like me to drive you to the hospital?" the officer asked.

"No. No, thank you," said Matthew. "I'll be fine. I'll have a scotch when I get home."

"Maybe a double wouldn't hurt," said the officer.

"Maybe not," said Matthew.

Matthew was immediately joined by Jordan and Sharon, and, a moment later, by Marika.

"Should I cancel your flight?" asked Sharon.

"No," said Matthew. "No. I'm okay. I'm glad I have something to focus on. Are *you* okay, Marika?"

"I'm fine," said Marika. "I've had worse tumbles playing volleyball. Seriously."

"Can I drive you home?" Jordan asked Matthew.

"No. I'm fine to take the subway. But thank. . . . I was bringing you a muffin, Sharon, but I dropped it somewhere."

"It's the last thing you should be worrying about," said Sharon. Jordan wordlessly handed Marika the small package he was holding.

None of the four felt disposed to say much more. Matthew and Sharon returned to their office, and Jordan and Marika to theirs. And a few moments after checking his email and packing up his laptop, Matthew left, pausing only to ask Sharon to lock up and leave early herself.

Chapter Four

Coming home to his sixth-floor condo on Gothic Avenue gave Matthew a sense of peace. The building was just steps from the High Park subway station, and he imagined his blood pressure dropping as he entered the brightly-lit lobby and exchanged greetings with the genial concierge, Mr. Naipaul. The elevator was swift and quiet, and if shared with other residents they were generally good humoured, and not inclined to launch into rambling monologues about the weather. When he unlocked his own door, he was usually greeted by Mr. Smudge, his large black-and-white Norwegian forest cat, a creature almost dog-like in his affection for his master. Matthew had, then, a reasonable expectation of finding an oasis of calm for a couple of hours, before venturing out again to collect a package of information from Andrew.

But Mr. Smudge did not greet him at the door. Matthew had to seek him out in the second bedroom—a room lined with bookshelves—and even then he wasn't in his bed, where Matthew suspected he spent a fair bit of time when he wasn't home, but huddled in a corner, his face turned to the wall. "What's wrong, Mr. Smudge?" Matthew asked, stroking his head. Mr. Smudge was shivering, though the temperature in the condo was comfortable, and it took Matthew picking him up, carrying him into the living room, and sitting him on his lap before he came back to himself. "Do I need to take you to the vet, Smudgie?" Matthew asked.

When, eventually, Mr. Smudge was purring and behaving normally, Matthew lifted him off his lap and fixed himself a scotch-and-soda. He checked his landline. While many of his younger acquaintances had given up on a home phone, Matthew had kept his. Only family and his closest friends had the number, so he was able to maintain a boundary between his personal and business lives. He had a message.

There was static on the line when the recording began—a detail that suggested that the call, which came from an unlisted number, was long-distance. "Maybe next time," a lightly-accented voice said. "Maybe next time, eh, Detective?" And then the click of a hang-up. Matthew played the message several times, trying each time to place the accent, then saved it and went to the window overlooking High Park. He stood there for several minutes, sipping his scotch and gazing out at the trees and at the Toronto folk entering into and exiting from the park. He'd received some strange calls over the years, but this one unsettled him more than any other—especially when juxtaposed with the accident just over an hour before, and Mr. Smudge's unusual behaviour. It wasn't simply strange: it was weird.

"How would you like some dinner?" he asked the cat. Mr. Smudge looked up from his place on the sofa, then headed to the kitchen. Matthew followed, rummaged for a can of tuna, and served up the evening meal, the cat drawing figure-eights around his knees as he worked. "There you go, Smudgie," he said. "Never say your daddy doesn't look after you." He watched for a moment or two, registering that Mr. Smudge's appetite was unimpaired, then made himself a grilled cheese and tomato sandwich.

While he ate, Matthew downloaded the photos Andrew had sent, and put them in a file labelled, simply, *Hannah*. He Googled her, finding plenty of leads to the young woman's life: a Facebook account whose wall was filled with expressions of shock and professions of love, mostly, so far as he could judge, from young women roughly her age; a LinkedIn profile revealing that she had a degree in Drama but was working as a waitress; a resume on Mandy.com showing that she had credits in several university and small-scale independent films. He watched her demo reel on YouTube a couple of times, recognizing that she had range and talent, and conscious too of the beauty and vitality which had so captivated Andrew.

Sharon had emailed him with his travel details, and Andrew had sent a message with a list of telephone numbers. *Good for you, lad*, he muttered, picking up a pen and paper and noting down the numbers for Hannah's parents, the manager at the restaurant where she worked, and a couple of women Andrew described as "close girlfriends." He called the parents' number. After a couple of rings, a woman's voice answered.

"Mrs. Hutchinson? My name is Matthew Harding. I'm a private investigator, and I've been hired by Andrew Greenfield to investigate the disappearance of your daughter. Do you have a minute to speak to me, or is this a bad time?"

There was a silence at the other end for a moment, then: "I can give you a minute, Mr. Harding."

"Thank you. Is there any possibility I could come and see you this evening? I appreciate that it's very short notice, but I have only just been engaged by Mr. Greenfield, and I'm flying to New Brunswick in the morning."

"This evening would not be possible," said the woman. "My husband and I have been"—her voice shook—"very upset. We're not seeing anyone except family. Not for a while. I don't know why Andrew has hired you, Mr. Harding. I mean, I'm grateful, but I don't see that there's anything you can do."

Matthew winced as he realized he had not asked Andrew whether he had told the Hutchinsons about the wedding video. He also saw, in that instant, that perhaps his own judgement had been impaired more than he'd thought by the car accident, and that he should not have called the parents without first asking Andrew what he'd told them.

"I completely understand. May I ask you one very difficult question?"

"I don't guarantee you an answer," she replied, "but you may ask."

"Thank you. Mrs. Hutchinson, if Hannah had somehow survived the event on the whale-watching boat, would she have any reason to want to disappear for a while? I guess I'm really asking whether her relationships here were happy ones." He scrunched up his face at how gauche his question must sound.

"We were very close, Mr. Harding," Mrs. Hutchinson said. "If Hannah had survived, she would absolutely have contacted her father and me. And she and Andrew were in love. She would have come home to all of us." Her voice broke. "I'm sorry. I must go. This is all still so fresh and painful."

"I'm so sorry, Mrs. Hutch—" but the phone had gone dead. *Idiot. You idiot,* Matthew thought. *Twenty-three years in the business and you screw up like a freaking amateur.* He thought about pouring another scotch-and-soda, but decided that would be rewarding himself for making a mistake, and *that* he could not do. He consoled himself by scratching behind Mr. Smudge's ears, pleasing the cat and calming himself in the process.

CHAPTER FIVE

Andrew lived in a two-floor apartment in a long, four-storey building that had once housed industrial warehouses. It was ugly from the outside, and very close to the road, but the size of the space and height of the ceilings went a long way toward compensating for the poor curb appeal. The ground-level was mostly taken up by an open concept studio in which there were four painting stations, each equipped with an easel and littered with canvases, brushes, artist palettes and tubes of oil, acrylic and water-colour paints.

"I share the studio with some friends. We split the rent," said Andrew, as Matthew looked around. "Hannah and I live upstairs. This way."

Matthew followed his client up a set of spiral metal stairs to Andrew's living room. The space was large by Toronto apartment standards, and the sofa, coffee table, two armchairs, and a television did not quite fill it. Some colourful abstract art hung on the walls, and the quality and colours of the curtains and rugs suggested that either Andrew or Hannah had good taste and a little money.

"So," Andrew said, "here are some more photos of Hannah. Recent ones. She's with her best friend Rebecca in this one. And that's another friend of hers, Nina. And these are her parents and, I think, her aunt."

"Excellent," said Matthew. "She's very photogenic. And she looks happy in all these."

Andrew nodded. "She was happy. Here's a note she wrote me a few months ago, so you can see what her handwriting looks like. Did you get my email with the telephone numbers?"

"I did," said Matthew. "And I need to ask you. Have you mentioned the video to her parents? Or to anyone else?"

"Not to her parents," said Andrew. "I don't know whether I should just yet. I only got it two days ago. Before that I just assumed . . ."

"I understand," said Matthew. "Have you shown it to any of her friends?"

"Yes, to Rebecca Ostroff," said Andrew, pointing at one of the pictures. "And to my brother, Luke. And to Nina Brown." Again, he pointed.

"And who sent you the video?"

"His name's Russell. Russell Gregory," said Andrew. "He lives in Edmonton."

"With all the millions of videos on YouTube," asked Matthew, "does it strike you as odd that Russell should have come across one from Mexico that features your fiancée?"

"Yes," said Andrew. "I thought so. But Russell's a drama teacher. He told me that he was investigating wedding rituals from different cultures when he came across the video. When he wrote to me, he didn't say, 'This is Hannah.' He said, 'you know, this looks *like* Hannah.' He's never met her—just seen photographs of us on my Facebook page."

"Where do you know Russell from?" Matthew asked.

"From university," said Andrew. "Eight years ago. Nine."

"Okay," said Matthew. "I think I have everything I need for now. Is there anything else?"

"How much do you charge if you're successful?" asked Andrew. "I mean, I have access to money, but I'm not wealthy. I need to know if I should be fundraising, or taking out a loan, or, I don't know . . ." He trailed off. Then: "I'll do whatever it takes."

"Before I spend all the $10,000 you've given me, I'll tell you how much more, if anything, I need to continue. I may conclude that there's nothing I can do for you, in which case I'll refund anything over and above my expenses. If I find her, I'll keep anything over my expenses as my fee. Does that seem fair?"

"More than fair," said Andrew.

"May I ask what you do for a living?" asked Matthew.

"I'm an art forger," said Andrew, "but not the criminal kind. I'm part of a collective with three friends, and we produce paintings in the style of various famous artists, and sell them to enthusiasts on the understanding that they won't be sold on as originals. At the moment I'm specializing in the style of a British Victorian artist called Edwin Long. Would you like to see some of my work?"

"Very much," said Matthew.

The two of them descended the stairs, and Andrew led the way to one of the work stations. On the easel was a detailed sketch of a nativity scene. The baby was in a manger lined with hay, while his mother looked down on him lovingly, reaching out a hand to smooth his blanket. A bearded man was in the background opening the stable door, and a richly dressed fellow in Persian dress was entering. He, the Persian, carried a small gold box.

"Long painted portraits, but he had a particular interest in illustrating biblical scenes," said Andrew. "As far as we know he never painted a nativity. I've studied his work, and I'm trying to paint the nativity as he might have painted it, if he'd been moved to do so. Or commissioned."

"I'm impressed," said Matthew, studying the sketch. "And is there a market for, what would you call them—honest forgeries?"

"Yes," said Andrew. "You need to have a dealer with access to people who have the money for this kind of thing, but if you're good at what you do you can make a reasonable living. I only began a year ago, but my stuff is beginning to sell. One of the guys in here has been at it for six years now, and he's making enough to afford a down payment on a house."

"That's saying something in Toronto," said Matthew.

"You're not kidding," said Andrew. "Hannah and I were doing okay, but we figured we'd be renting for the next ten years anyway. And maybe forever."

"I see that Hannah was in some movies," said Matthew. "Did they pay well?"

"God, no," said Andrew. "If she was really lucky, she'd make $100, $150 a day—and she'd have to take time off from waitressing to do it, so she really lost money when she was filming."

"She did well as a waitress?"

"She's a beautiful blonde," said Andrew. "She could make $350 in tips on a good Saturday night. She was paying all the rent when we moved in here. It's fifty/fifty now. Well . . . it was."

Matthew extended his hand. "I'm flying out to New Brunswick tomorrow morning," he said. "I'll be speaking with the captain of the whale-watching boat, and with the RCMP officer who headed up the investigation. I'll probably poke my nose around a bit more while I'm there, then I'll head down to Mexico. You can expect an email from me when I leave New Brunswick, and another when I've found my bearings in Huajuapan. And, of course, you can email me any time, though I can't promise an instant response."

"Okay," said Andrew. "Thank you for taking this on."

"Thank you for trusting me with it," said Matthew. "If Hannah is alive, I'll do my best to find her."

CHAPTER SIX

Matthew left Andrew's apartment and headed to the street-car stop. As he walked, he found himself thinking with surprising intensity about the sketch Andrew had showed him. It was just a pencil sketch, but there was a vibrancy, a buzzing alive-ness, in the figures that had deeply impressed him. He was not familiar with the work of Edwin Long, but Matthew thought that the picture might well stand on its own merits. He imagined it hanging in the room with his shelves of books about religion and spirituality.

There was only one other person at the streetcar stop when he arrived, a male teenager of either Chinese or Korean ancestry. He stood maybe five foot five, and wore the universal uniform of young Canadian males—blue jeans, runners, a ball cap, and, as a variation on the theme, an oversized Raptors t-shirt with num-ber 16 on the front. He had a skateboard, too, and his right foot was pushing the board back and forth, back and forth.

Matthew often saw skateboarders in High Park and else-where in Toronto, and he usually found them agreeable. He was puzzled by the large loops some of them stuck in their earlobes, and irritated when they zipped along the sidewalks populated with seniors or small children, but he had no quarrel with kids who wanted to get around the city without driving cars or motorcycles. "Hi," he said, nodding to the boy.

"Hey," said the boy, and he took his right foot off the board. Something in the way his body tensed, however, alerted Matthew that he was under threat, so when the boy suddenly brought his foot down on the back edge of the board, flipping it in the air, Matthew took a full step back. The boy grabbed the board as it spun up and in the same motion swung at Matthew, missing him by less than an inch. Matthew, who'd done some martial arts training over the years, struck a defensive posture and prepared for the boy to come back at him . . . but he didn't. He followed through on his lunge at Matthew, spinning around with some grace, turned to face the detective, then, seeing that he was unfazed and poised, curled his lip in a sneer. "Maybe next time," he said, turned away, and headed down Broadview on his board at high speed.

Matthew watched him go with a mixture of anger and shock. The boy had used the same words as had been left in the telephone message, though the voice was not the same. *Maybe next time.* Matthew was not an anxious man, but he recognized that he now had strong grounds for thinking that someone, or some group, was targeting him. Had that car on Prospect Avenue been aiming at *him*?

Back at his condo Andrew reflected that his specialty, *cases with a metaphysical dimension*, meant that he had avoided many of the common hazards of private eyes—spouses angry at being photographed *in flagrante delicto* with illicit lovers, husbands trying to evade alimony and child support payments, and break-and-enter specialists determined not to be identified. But twenty-three years in practice had brought him into conflict with dishonest psychics, unscrupulous televangelists and twisted cult leaders, and several of them had turned violent, or unleashed violent subordinates on him. Matthew had fended off knife attacks twice, been shot at several times, and assaulted with fists and feet more times than he could count. But to be aimed at with a car, implicitly threatened in a phone call, and assaulted with a skateboard in the space of a few hours represented an unlikely and sinister sequence of events.

He called his neighbour, Steven, who had often fed Mr. Smudge breakfast and dinner, cleaned his box, and spent some time with him. Steven's big heart and unstructured schedule meant that he was happy to care for the cat for the next fortnight, if necessary. It didn't hurt that Matthew left a 750-ml bottle of rye, and a shot glass, on the sideboard when he went away. With success on this front, Matthew resolved to make one further phone call—this one to Hannah's friend Rebecca.

"Hello." A pleasant but somewhat muffled female voice on the other end. Matthew had the sense that she was probably cupping her mouth as she spoke.

"Rebecca Ostroff? My name is Matthew Harding. I've been hired by Andrew Greenfield to investigate the disappearance of Hannah Hutchinson. Do you have a moment to speak with me?"

"Can I call you back in about five minutes, Mr. Harding? I'm in a rehearsal hall at the moment, and I need to go outside."

"Of course. Thank you." Matthew put his phone down and went off in search of his passport and a Spanish phrase book. His phone rang a few minutes later.

"Ms. Ostroff?"

"Hi. Andrew told me you might call."

"And he also told you about the YouTube video?"

"Yes, I've watched it. It's Hannah."

"There's no doubt in your mind?"

"None at all. It's Hannah. I'd know her anywhere."

"Well, in a real sense that's good news, because it means she survived. But it also presents us with a mystery. Ms. Ostroff, can—"

"Please, call me Rebecca."

"Rebecca, can you think of *any* reason why Hannah might not want to reveal to anyone that she survived the accident? Any reason—no matter how far-fetched?"

"I've asked myself that question a hundred times in the last two days," she replied, "and the only possible reason I can think of is that she hit her head and lost her memory. It doesn't make sense otherwise. She and Andrew were so happy—and she was close to her parents, too. And she has many friends here."

"She never confided to you that she and Andrew were having problems? I'm not suggesting at all that this was the case, you understand—"

"No," Rebecca said firmly. "They were very happy together. And there was no one else."

"I thought as much, but I had to ask," said Matthew. "And what about the man beside her in the video? Do you recognize him from anywhere?"

"No. He certainly wasn't in our circle of friends here. And she doesn't look happy to be with him."

"No, she doesn't," Matthew said. "Thank you for this."

"What are you going to do now?"

"I'm off to New Brunswick in the morning—and then on to Mexico from there. I want to move as quickly as possible."

"Please do everything you can," said Rebecca. "Hannah is loved by a lot of people."

"I promise I will," said Matthew.

CHAPTER SEVEN

Matthew fell asleep quickly, but slipped into a dream which, in its vividness and coherence, was unlike any he had experienced before. It was night, and he found himself walking along a narrow, dusty street lined with small, two-storey stone houses. There were few people about, and what little light there was came from the half moon and the stars—one of which seemed particularly brilliant. He was conscious that he was about a stone's throw behind a man on a horse, and that the man was turning his head from side to side as if he were trying to get his bearings or, perhaps, looking for something, or someplace, or someone. It is difficult to gauge the passage of time in a dream, but it seemed to Matthew that only a moment or two passed before the horseman fixed his gaze on a particular house and reined in his mount. The rider fumbled with a bag attached to his saddle, detached it, then dismounted. He dropped the reins, said something in a low voice to the horse, then stepped up to the door of the house, hesitated a moment, then knocked.

At the instant the horseman knocked, Matthew was distracted by a door opening onto the street from the house to his right. A figure emerged—a broad-shouldered young man with short dark hair, and with neither beard nor moustache. He had small ears and a big nose. He was carrying what looked very much like a brick. This young man started when he saw Matthew, almost recoiling. He looked back into the house, as if for guidance, then turned back to Matthew. "You don't belong here," he hissed. "Go away. GO AWAY." He drew back his arm, and threw the brick.

And Matthew woke up, wide-eyed, dry-mouthed, and with an urgent need to urinate. He shook his head, got up, made his way into the bathroom, and glanced down at his feet. They were covered in a thin layer of dust.

CHAPTER EIGHT

Matthew's alarm rang at 5:00 a.m. He had forty-five minutes to get ready, then it was off to Union Station to catch the Express to the airport. His bag was already packed, so getting ready consisted largely of shaving, showering, and downing some breakfast.

The Air Canada flight took a little less than two hours: Matthew read Elaine Pagels' *Why Religion?* for the first hour, glancing out the window occasionally as eastern Ontario and western Quebec unspooled below, then slept until the plane began its descent into Saint John. Sharon had booked him a rental car, and the young woman behind the desk said cheerfully, "Welcome to New Brunswick—the friendly province!"

St. Andrew's-by-the-Sea, the point of departure for Andrew and Hannah's ill-fated boat trip, looked radiant in the early afternoon sun. Matthew admired the turn-of-the-century houses and tree-lined streets, and breathed in the salty sea air with a kind of gratitude. He had worried, briefly, when he saw that Sharon had booked him a room at the Algonquin Resort—he had no desire to be profligate with Andrew's money—but the cost of a small room at the Algonquin was roughly what he'd have paid for a fleabag motel in Toronto.

He tipped the young man who showed him to his room, explored it briefly, then consulted the services directory for the names of whale-watching tours, finding the one he wanted immediately. He made an online reservation for the following morning. This accomplished, he made a phone call to a contact he had in town, a private investigator he'd helped out with a case that had spread its tentacles into Ontario. "Lloyd," he said, "I need help getting a meeting with the RCMP officer who headed up the investigation into the rogue wave drownings in June."

Four o'clock in the afternoon saw Matthew sitting across the desk from a polite but sceptical RCMP Inspector. Dwayne Arsenault, a florid-faced man in his early fifties, twisted his wedding ring obsessively as he addressed his visitor. "Lloyd tells me you have some new information on Hannah Hutchinson," he said.

"I have," Matthew said. "Do you have a photo of the young lady?"

The Inspector opened a file, and pulled out a glossy photograph. "Her parents sent us this," he said. "It seems to be some sort of theatre head-shot."

Matthew nodded, then passed his cell phone across the desk. "This was posted *after* the whaling-boat accident," he said.

The Inspector watched for ten seconds, then looked up at Matthew. "What am I looking at?" he asked.

"It's a wedding video taken in Mexico," said Matthew. "You're going to see Hannah in about fifteen seconds."

Arsenault gave a tiny jerk of his head. He watched to the end, then replayed it, freezing on Hannah. "Well, it looks like her," he said, "but can we be sure? Have her parents confirmed it is?"

"Her parents haven't seen this," said Matthew, "but her fiancé gave it to me, and *he* says it's her—and her closest girlfriend confirms it."

"How do we know this wasn't taken before early June?"

"She's wearing a brooch Greenfield bought for her here in New Brunswick."

The Inspector whistled through his teeth. "Well, that's a twist."

"It is," said Matthew. "I've been hired by Andrew to see if I can find Hannah. Do you mind if I ask you a couple of questions?"

Arsenault thought for a moment. "I'll answer you off the record," he said. "Understood? I'm not fully comfortable with the fact that the parents haven't seen this. And it's awkward that you're a PI rather than a cop. No offense."

"No offense taken," said Matthew. "Did it surprise you that Ms. Hutchinson's body was not recovered?"

"No," said the Inspector. "The ocean is vast, and the currents are strong. We felt we were fortunate to recover five of the six missing."

"Were many boats involved in the recovery operation?"

"There were two coast guard vessels deployed, and all sorts of ordinary citizens up and down the coast came out to help. There's a real community spirit in this province—particularly in the small towns."

Matthew smiled, remembering the cheery greeting at the airport. "I believe it," he said. "Can you think of any other occasion when someone has gone missing in a boating accident, only to turn up somewhere else weeks or months later?"

"Not in any case I've worked on." Arsenault slid Matthew's phone back across the desk.

"And do you have any reason to believe that there are people-traffickers, or smugglers, working along this stretch of coast?"

The Inspector thought for a moment. "Yes," he said. "We've had some experience with people smuggling in illegal weapons from the States. That's an ongoing issue. And a couple of years back we had some girls from Eastern Europe brought in from New York State. Prostitutes."

"But no instances of young women being taken outside the country from New Brunswick?"

"Not to my knowledge, no. No." He picked up Hannah's head shot and looked at it hard. "But she's a beautiful young lady." He left the thought hanging.

"She is that," said Matthew. "Just one final question: did you find anything at all during the search that struck you as unexpected—strange?"

"Maybe," the inspector said, "but I doubt it's the kind of thing you have in mind."

"I don't have any preconceptions," said Matthew. "I'm fishing in uncharted waters."

"When the first Coast Guard vessel arrived," Arsenault said, "they found the water in the immediate area around the boat weirdly calm, except for a whirlpool about ninety, one hundred metres from the wreckage. The whirlpool disappeared a few minutes after they got there, but the captain said it was a bit . . . eerie."

"Eerie," Matthew repeated.

"Yup." Arsenault twisted his wedding ring furiously.

"Thank you, Inspector." Matthew shifted his weight into the back of his chair.

"You're welcome. What are your plans? Where do you go from here?"

"I'm flying down to Mexico—to a little town called Huajuapan, where this video was taken. It's in the state of Oaxaca."

"Could I ask you for a copy of the video?" The Inspector took a card from his drawer and placed it beside Matthew's cell.

"I'll send you the link," said Matthew. He picked up his phone and the card, rose, and offered Arsenault his hand. "It was good meeting you."

Arsenault stood up, and shook Matthew's hand. "Maybe you could let me know if you find anything—or if you need help. We have limited resources, but we do what we can."

"I will," said Matthew.

"And look me up if you come back to St. Andrew's," said the Inspector. "Maybe next time we could get a beer somewhere."

"I would like—" Matthew began. Then stopped. *Maybe next time? Am I going mad?* he thought. "It would be a pleasure," he said, and left the detachment office with a welter of questions and anxieties swirling in his mind.

CHAPTER NINE

At the age of forty-six, Matthew had ceased to feel all that comfortable taking his shirt off in public. He was certainly not obese, but he was no longer slender either—and while he had a reasonably defined musculature, he also had a scar from a knife attack across his chest that tended to attract attention. But the day was still warm, and the sun was still shining, so he went for a swim in the Algonquin pool. There were enough children and adults swimming haphazardly that doing lengths soon became impractical, so Matthew contented himself with swimming breaststroke around them, smiling at toddlers in their water wings or parents' arms, and occasionally scowling at teenage boys who insisted on splashing or kicking without any regard for who was nearby. He swam for a quarter of an hour, then hoisted himself out of the water, found a deck chair to recline in, wrapped himself in a towel, and gradually closed his eyes. After a few minutes, however, he became conscious of a shadow covering his upper body, and he opened his eyes again.

A woman—black, perhaps fifty years old—was smiling down at him. "Is this chair reserved for anyone?" she asked.

"No, not at all," said Matthew. "Please help yourself."

"My name is Clara," said the woman, lowering herself into the chair. "I'm on a working holiday here in St. Andrew's." Her diction was somewhat formal, and she had an accent Matthew could not quite place, but there was something about her that disarmed suspicion. Matthew raised the back of his chair so he could talk more comfortably. "I don't want to interrupt your sunbathing," said Clara.

"You're not," said Matthew. "Tanning has never been a priority for me."

"I think it must have been a priority for my distant ancestors," said Clara—and she laughed. "But that's a very Lamarkian thing for me to say."

"What's the working part of your holiday?" asked Matthew.

"There's a clergy conference just up the road at St. Stephen—at the university there," said Clara. "A wonderful setting for a wonderful gathering."

"Are you a member of the clergy yourself?"

"I'm a minister in the Anglican Church," she said. "My home parish is in Ontario, so this is a bit of a holiday for me. Oh, yes."

Trinidad? thought Matthew, fixing on the verbal tic. *Guyana?* "I'm from Toronto," he said.

"I know, Matthew," said Clara, laughing again. "You have the look of a Torontonian about you."

Matthew was a little tired after his early departure from Toronto and the stress of travelling, but he was not asleep. "How is it you know my name, Clara?" he asked politely.

"Oh, my," said Clara, "if you didn't tell me, I must have guessed. Or perhaps it was simply a kind of intuition—like knowing you were from Toronto. . . . Isn't she beautiful?" A striking brunette in a skimpy green bikini had just passed between them and the pool. Arrested though he'd been by Clara's use of his name, Matthew had noticed her. Every man on the pool deck had.

"She is," said Matthew, "but knowing my name requires a little more than intuition."

"I'm glad you're wide awake, Matthew," said Clara, "because you'll need to be. You're heading into deep water . . . and there are monsters just below the surface."

Matthew was silent for a moment. "You know who I'm looking for?"

"Oh, yes. You're looking for Hannah Hutchinson."

"And you're not a minister, are you?"

"I *am* a minister—but my responsibilities are a little unusual. I help out with challenges like the one you're facing." Clara looked him directly in the eyes, all joviality gone—and yet there was kindness there.

"Okay," said Matthew. "I'm not really sure what you mean, but I'm always grateful for help. Do you have any advice for me?"

"Yes," said Clara. "What you're facing isn't hypothetical or figurative. It's literal. It's real. I'm talking about *evil*, Matthew— a very specific kind of evil. Don't underestimate it. But don't for a moment believe that you are alone, or that the cause is hopeless. And Matthew: sometimes we do some of our most important work when we're asleep. You need to stay focused even then."

Matthew stared at her, at once bewildered and, weirdly, comforted. At that instant a hotel employee, a bell-boy in a green uniform, came up to them. "Reverend Clara," he said, "you have a telephone call at the front desk."

"Oh, my," said Clara, rising from her chair with unexpected grace. "In my line of work, Matthew, as in yours, one is always on call. You have a good evening. God bless." And she was gone.

Matthew gazed after her, then surveyed the pool deck. He scanned the people still swimming—their numbers dwindling as the dinner hour approached. Finally, he looked across the pool at the people, like himself, sitting in deck chairs, and just for a moment wondered if an East Asian teenager wearing a ball cap might possibly be the youth with a skateboard who had assaulted him at the streetcar stop. *Don't be daft, Matthew,* he thought. *Focus on what's real.* And with that idea firmly in his mind he got up, slipped into his flip-flops, and headed back to his room.

CHAPTER TEN

Sleep did not come easily. Whether it was the unfamiliarity of his bed, or the lamb stew he had eaten at supper, Matthew stayed awake for a good hour after switching the lights off. Part of the problem, certainly, was the voices and images in his head—the message on his answering service, the sneer of the skateboarding teen, the blank face of the street person pinned between the car's bumper and the storefront. An imagined picture of the whirlpool in the ocean disturbed him too, and he found himself juxtaposing that with the memory of Inspector Arsenault twisting his wedding ring. Matthew got up for a while and tried to read Pagels, but he could not focus. He turned on the television, telling himself that he might watch a talk show, but he knew, as he flicked through the channels, that his real destination was a pornographic movie, and he watched as much of one as he needed to get the relief that was still, in his mid-40s, more powerful and insistent that he wanted to acknowledge even to himself. He had had several relationships since the death of his beloved wife eight years before, and he had entered those relationships out of a desire for sexual intimacy that destroyed his judgement and subverted his best intentions. Twenty-three hours of the day he was a reflective man obsessed with spiritual questions, but for one hour in twenty-four he was consumed by lust. As a kind of penance, he did ninety push-ups in three sets of thirty, then collapsed on the floor, feeling the burn in his muscles as a reproach to his level of fitness. He showered for the second time that day, and returned to bed.

Sleep, when it came, brought another vivid dream. It was again night, and Matthew was back in the same narrow, dusty street—and he realized, in the dream, that he was back: *I'm having a* lucid *dream,* he thought, and looked at his hands, conscious that this was a decision he had just made, that he had some degree of control in this dreamscape. The broad-shouldered young man was nowhere in sight, but the horseman up ahead was standing at the door of the house where he had knocked, and as Matthew watched he removed a shiny box from the bag he was carrying, and cradled it in his hands. A moment later the door opened from within, and the horseman gave a slight bow and entered the house, disappearing from Matthew's sight. Matthew stood in the street for a moment, unsure what he should do, then he felt a gentle, welcoming summons and began walking down the street toward the house. At the instant he began walking, a door to a house between him and his destination opened, and, improbably, but true to the logic of dreams, the broad-shouldered man emerged accompanied by the East Asian teenager. They advanced to the middle of the street and stood waiting for him. Matthew kept walking . . . and as he walked, he was conscious that there was someone at his right shoulder, walking beside him.

"Hello again, Matthew," Reverend Clara said.

"Clara!" he said. "You're here, too?" He stopped and faced her.

"Oh, yes," she said, stopping too. "And I have something for you." He saw she was carrying a wooden staff, perhaps three feet in length, and she handed it to him. "It may be useful," she said, and disappeared.

Matthew accepted the disappearance. It seemed logical enough in the dream, and he turned and faced the two figures in the middle of the street. It struck him that they shifted uneasily when they saw he now had something he could use as a weapon. Matthew walked towards them again.

"That thing won't help you," said the broad-shouldered man.

"Let's hope I won't need to use it, then," said Matthew, "Please move aside."

"Big man with a stick," said the teenager.

"Yes," said Matthew. "But there are two of you. Please move aside."

Yet another door opened to his left, and Matthew was aware of an intoxicatingly sweet scent of musk and vanilla and cinnamon.

He took his eyes off his two antagonists and saw a woman remarkably like the beautiful brunette from the hotel pool standing in the street. She was wearing what looked like a long cloth shirt, but as she stood there, she began seductively to raise the garment. "Matthew," she said, "look what I have for you—"

A blow to his head, and a fall toward blackness . . . and then he woke up. He reached up to his forehead where, he sensed, he had been struck in the dream, and he felt a sticky wetness there before falling helplessly back to sleep.

CHAPTER ELEVEN

There was a little blood on the pillow the next morning. Matthew got ready for the day, then ran a basin of cold water and put the pillowcase in to soak before going down to breakfast. He tended the cut on his forehead with antibiotic ointment, and ran his fingers gently over the bruise. It made no sense. It made no sense at all.

He ordered a cheese omelette with whole wheat toast, and read the paper while he ate. His waitress refilled his coffee cup and, at his request, brought him marmalade. "I'm sorry," she said, "we usually have it on the table." She was a slim lass, pretty, red-haired, and probably a university student working for the summer, Matthew thought.

"Are you from St. Andrew's?" he asked.

"No, I'm from Fredericton," she said. "I'm a student at UNB."

"What are you studying?"

"History. I'm a bit of a dinosaur."

"Why do you say that?"

"Subjects like history and English aren't as popular as when you went to school," she said, putting a few extra creamers beside his cup.

"I never went to university," Matthew said, a little sadly. "What are students taking now?"

"Business," she said. "Everyone wants to do business. Or computers. Or gender studies. It's like there are different tribes on campus. Did you go to college instead?"

"Yes," said Matthew. "But just a three-month program. I wish I had gone."

"I'm sure you made the right choice for you," she said. "I'll graduate with a mountain of debt and no job to go to—at least, not in my field. My dad thinks I'm crazy."

"What about teaching?"

"No jobs for history teachers," she said. "I'd spend five or six years on the supply list—if I could even get on it in the first place. You could always go back, you know."

"Go back?"

"To school. You could take courses part-time."

"Well, that's true," said Matthew.

She smiled at him. "You have a good day," she said, touching his shoulder, then flitted away to another table. He watched her go with a mixture of loneliness, human warmth, and, yes, frank lust—and left a generous tip.

★ ★ ★

Matthew set out to walk to the dock from which the whale-watching vessel was to depart. The weather was gorgeous, and he welcomed the opportunity to stretch his legs. He arrived half an hour later, sweating a little, but grateful for the exercise and the fresh air. It was another half hour before boarding was allowed, but he made his way to the ticket booth in hopes that the attendant might tell him how and when to speak to the captain.

The woman in the booth was middle-aged, and had the kind of pinched expression that suggested a powerful migraine. "One or two?" she asked.

"I've already booked," said Matthew, holding up his phone screen to show her.

"I don't need to see it," she said brusquely. "They'll check on the boat."

"Okay," said Matthew, "but I have a question. Is it possible to speak with the captain before we set out?"

"Why?"

"I want to ask him about the day the rogue wave hit."

"Are you a journalist? We don't speak to journalists."

"No," said Matthew. He took a twenty-dollar bill from his wallet and slid it across the counter. "This is for your trouble," he said. The attendant said nothing, but she took the bill—and became significantly more amenable.

"The captain who was on duty then had a kind of nervous breakdown," she said. "He was really upset that people died."

"I'm sure he was," said Matthew.

"Like, the whole boat was knocked over. Customers were swept over the side."

"Do you know where the captain is?" asked Matthew. "Does he live here in St. Andrew's?"

"He's gone to Mexico for a holiday. Like, to recover."

"To Mexico," said Matthew. "Have you any idea where in Mexico?"

"No," said the woman. "Somewhere down there."

Well, that narrows it down, Matthew thought—but did not say. "Is any other member of the crew from that day scheduled to be on the vessel today?"

"Yeah, the captain," said the woman. "Like, she was the first officer that day, but now she's the captain. They promoted her."

"Do you think the captain might speak with me?" asked Matthew.

"Maybe I could phone her."

Matthew took another twenty out of his wallet. "I'd be so grateful if you would," he said.

The woman picked up her cell phone, turned her back on Matthew, and made a brief phone call. Turning back to him she said, "She'll talk to you on the boat, when they're underway. She knows what you look like. She'll see you from the wheelhouse when you get on."

"Thank you," said Matthew; he smiled tightly, and left the dock for the shore. He took the next little while to walk along the St. Andrew's waterfront, savouring the sights and smells of a small seaside port: the gulls wheeling, the sun sparkling off the water, the rich, redolent scents of salt, seaweed, and fish. When he returned to the dock, there were a few people waiting in a good-humoured line that started a couple of yards back from the ticket-booth.

"Lady in there said we have to line up here," a hearty gentleman in his sixties remarked as Matthew came up behind him and his wife.

"She made us feel real welcome," said the wife—but she laughed in a way that suggested she was more amused than annoyed.

"I talked with her earlier," said Matthew. "Maybe not the best ambassador for the company."

"They should hire her as a border guard," said the gentleman. "No one'd get past her."

"Are you Americans?" Matthew asked, guessing that they almost certainly were.

"We're visiting from Idaho," said the wife, and the three of them fell into a pleasant but inconsequential conversation as, over the next fifteen minutes, about twenty other people straggled up to join the line forming behind them.

"If this is everyone, the boat won't be full," observed the American gentleman.

"Lots of competition in the area," said Matthew.

"And this is the company whose boat got hit by that big wave," said the wife.

Matthew nodded.

"Well, I guess that means it's some other company's turn to get hit! Hey? Hey?" said the husband, laughing. "Thunder don't hit twice!"

"Lightning, dear," said the wife. Matthew did his best to compose his features in a way that suggested mirth.

"I'm hoping we see some whales," he said.

"Is that what this boat is for?" said the gentleman from Idaho. "I was hoping we'd see some nekkid mermaids!"

"Oh, Jerry," said the wife. And at that moment, mercifully, the woman from the ticket booth stepped out and signalled that they could all begin boarding.

CHAPTER TWELVE

In four minutes, everyone was on board. The young woman checking tickets simply glanced at Matthew's cell phone, suggesting that she either had very sharp eyes, or that she trusted he wasn't trying to steal a ride. Another crew member, a tanned young man, stood behind her, sizing people up and handing each passenger a life belt theoretically corresponding to his or her weight. The boat itself had two decks: there was a cabin with a sign indicating that its capacity was forty-eight passengers, and a rooftop outdoor viewing area. The wheelhouse, Matthew noticed, was set inside the cabin, right at the front and elevated a little. Though the sun was hot, he was reluctant to go inside the cabin immediately, so he went to the bow and watched the preparations to leave. He was joined by a solid-looking man in his early fifties. "Nothing like the smell of the sea," this fellow said.

"It's true," said Matthew. At that moment the engines throbbed to life beneath them, and the tanned young man, now on the dock, began unmooring the bow and the stern lines. He moved efficiently, jumping back onto the boat just as it edged away from its berth.

"Good summer job," said Matthew's companion.

"It beats some of the things I did," said Matthew.

"Joseph," said the solid-looking fellow, extending his hand. "Matthew."

The boat's public address system crackled: "This is Captain Sue. Welcome aboard. I have to ask you to wear your life-belts today as a precautionary measure. If you have any trouble getting yours on, please ask a crew member for assistance. We'll be out into the Bay of Fundy in about twelve minutes, and while it's a beautiful day you may find the water a little choppier than it is here. Oh, and Lisa has asked me to tell you that the snack bar will be open in five minutes."

"Captain Sue, eh?" said Joseph. "Let's hope she knows what she's doing."

Matthew did not respond to this, contenting himself with the pleasant sight of more and more of St. Andrew's coming into view as the boat moved further away from shore. It was a beautiful place, and he could easily understand why so many people wax eloquent about the Maritimes. He wondered, idly, what it might cost to rent a cottage there for a month. Close the office. Give Sharon a holiday. He could afford it. Sharon. He found, to his surprise, that he rather missed her.

"I'm gonna get a coffee," said Joseph. "Can I get you one?"

"No, thank you," said Matthew. Joseph moved off, and Matthew stared down at the water which, on this late morning, was an astonishingly light blue, dappled with sparkling sun spots. He was standing there almost mesmerized when the tanned young man approached him.

"The captain will see you, sir," he said. "She's in the wheelhouse." He gestured towards the cabin.

"Great. Thank you," said Matthew, and a moment later knocked at the wheelhouse door.

"Open," said a strong female voice, and Matthew opened the door to see a robust woman in her late twenties standing in front of a wheel just a little larger than one might find in a luxury car. There were certainly more gauges and controls than such a car would have, but Matthew's impression was of a fairly sleek dashboard. "One question," said the woman. "Are you a journalist?"

"No," said Matthew. "I'm a private investigator."

"Are you working for an insurance company?'

"No. I'm working for the fiancé of Hannah Hutchinson."

The woman hesitated for a moment, but then said, "okay. Come in."

Matthew entered. The captain glanced at him—her eyes a brilliant green—then looked back at the sea. "My name's Matthew Harding," said Matthew.

"I know," said the captain. "I can give you four minutes."

"Fair enough," said Matthew, closing the door behind him. "Can you tell me what you saw when the wave hit?"

"You realize I've told the police all this?"

"Yes. I'm working for Mr. Greenfield. He's . . . distraught."

Captain Sue nodded, took a breath. "The day was much like today," she said. "Bright, sunny sky. A bit of a swell out in the Bay, but nothing remarkable. And that's what *was* weird, because rogue waves usually come along when the sea is already rough, and they come at an angle to the wave flow." She took her hands off the helm briefly to illustrate.

"Can you guess how high it was?" asked Matthew.

"Forty feet," said the captain. "It was a monster—a wall of water. I've never seen anything like it. I hope I never see anything like it again. We stood no chance."

"And the captain did what he needed to do?"

"Are you sure you don't work for insurance?" She looked at Matthew suspiciously.

"I swear," said Matthew. "I have zero interest in liability. My client just wants a clear picture of what happened."

"The Captain had no time to do anything," said Captain Sue. "One moment the sea was calm—the next . . . we were swamped. The boat was literally tossed around: we spun 160, 180 degrees. Anyone out on the deck was swept into the water."

"The boat was knocked over?" said Matthew.

"On its side, you mean? No. But it could have been so easily."

"The lady at the ticket booth said it was."

"She wasn't on board," said Captain Sue, with some irritation. "Jesus, I hate it when people say things that aren't true."

"Okay," said Matthew. "Did you see Ms. Hutchinson go overboard?"

"I saw a number of people swept off the deck, but they were just flying figures to me. I hadn't talked with any of them. I don't mean I didn't care. I just mean that I hadn't really met any of them. I didn't know who Hannah was."

"I understand," said Matthew. "So you didn't see her in the water after the wave hit? A blonde woman—a few years younger than you are."

"When I picked myself up, I went out on the deck right away and began throwing life belts into the water," said Captain Sue. "I helped five people back up on the boat, but obviously she wasn't one of them. I don't remember seeing her at all."

"So you didn't see her sucked into the whirlpool?" said Matthew.

"The whole whirlpool business is just too weird for me," said the captain. "You don't get whirlpools with rogue waves. They're different things."

"But there was one?" said Matthew.

"Yes. There was. It started up a couple of minutes after the wave hit, and it kept swirling away until the rescue boats arrived. It was a distance from our boat, but we figure some of the people who drowned were sucked into it. I don't know. I really don't know." Captain Sue stared ahead, and Matthew thought she might be fighting back tears.

"This isn't the boat that was hit, is it?" he asked.

"Christ, no," said the captain. "Look, you have to go now. I need to concentrate on my job."

"I appreciate your time," said Matthew.

"Enjoy the trip," said Captain Sue. And, yes, there were tears in her eyes.

CHAPTER THIRTEEN

They did see whales—three humpback and, more surprisingly, two pilot, the latter dark black with a rounded, bulging forehead and relatively short snout. Captain Sue announced via the public address system that it was a little unusual to see the pilot whales. Matthew took this on faith, simply feeling a sense of awe whenever any of the creatures breached the surface, revealing roughly half their bodies before crashing back down into the water. Some of his fellow passengers were moved to cheer when this happened. "It's like the ocean is on fire!" one little girl said excitedly to her parents, and though this was something of an overstatement, Matthew understood.

Even Jerry seemed to have forgotten about his 'nekkid mermaids.' "Man," he said, coming up behind Matthew, "It's not like seeing them on T.V. This is the real deal."

Matthew ordered a tea and sandwich from the snack bar. The tea was almost undrinkable—the water not brought to a boil, and the tea bag presented on the side of the cup—but the cheese and tomato sandwich was made with real cheese, thickly sliced, and with good, ripe tomatoes. With potato chips, it made a half-way decent meal. Matthew almost felt guilty about taking the three-hour trip as part of the working day. He tried to engage the tanned young man in conversation about the rogue wave, asking him where roughly it had hit in relation to the shore, but it seemed likely the crew had been instructed not to talk about it all. The young man said he hadn't been on board that day, though his demeanour suggested otherwise.

As the vessel approached its berth, Matthew deliberated over what he should do next. He could explore whether anyone had seen someone resembling Hannah back on shore after the wave hit, but he quickly dismissed the idea. It made more sense to get down to Mexico as soon as possible. As soon as the boat docked, he checked the Air Canada website, and discovered that he could fly out that evening. He booked a ticket while standing on the dock, other passengers maneuvering around him as he punched in his credit card number. He then checked his email, finding a message from Sharon. "Hey, Matthew," it read. "The police asked me if you moved the car that hit the street guy. I don't think it's going to be a problem, but I thought I should give you a heads-up . . ." He swore under his breath. *I turned the damn engine off*, he thought, *and the car slipped back maybe two-and-a-half centimeters. It probably took some pressure off the poor bastard's ribs and heart.* That's *not what killed him.* Would someone really make an issue of that? But he knew someone could, if he or she felt bloody-minded enough. There was a follow-up email from Sharon: "I told them I didn't remember. It was a confusing moment." *You're a good lass*, Matthew thought.

He walked back to the hotel. It was hot now—too hot to really enjoy the walk, without the benefit of a strong breeze coming off the water. Still, he knew that he would remember this fondly in six months, when the days were short and grey and the thermometer read twenty below. His skin sucked in the sun, and his lungs drank in the sea air, and he was content, if not comfortable, in spite of Sharon's first email, and in spite of the mystery that made this trip necessary.

Back at the hotel, he stopped by the desk in the lobby and advised them he would be checking out in an hour. The clerk seemed a little taken aback: "Is anything wrong, sir?" she asked.

"Nothing at all," said Matthew. "Something came up and I have to fly out of the country this evening. But I hope to be back one day." He showered, repacked his suitcase, and sat down to send an email to Andrew. He copied Sharon and clicked send. On the day of the wave, the weather had been idyllic. The wave had come out of nowhere. A whirlpool had formed shortly after it hit. The sharp-eyed first officer, as she then was, had not seen Hannah in the water. The previous captain was now apparently in Mexico . . . And on top of it all, he, Matthew, was having some remarkably strange and vivid dreams. He shook his head, got up, did a last quick check of his room, then surrendered his key card at the front desk. He wanted a coffee, and resolved he would stop at a Timmy's—if St. Andrew's had a Timmy's—as he headed out of town.

On his way to the door, Matthew was intercepted by Reverend Clara, who sailed through the door as he approached it.

"Well, hello, Matthew," she said. "What a beautiful sunny day we are having!"

"It is that," he said, smiling. "A little hot, but . . ."

"Mexico is even hotter," said Clara. "Be sure you invest in a good sun hat."

"How on earth did you know—" Matthew began.

"And Matthew," Clara interjected, "Bethlehem is even hotter. You need to keep your wits about you. You really do need to stay focused."

"I'm not going to Bethlehem," said Matthew, still wondering how Clara could know about Mexico.

Clara laughed. "There's a sense," she said, "in which we are all going to Bethlehem, every one of us. I think," she added, "that we will see each other again. Oh, yes. I think so. Drive carefully." And she went on her way, waving gaily to the clerk behind the lobby desk, and calling out a greeting to the concierge.

Chapter Fourteen

The flight to Mexico City left at 7:00 p.m., so Matthew made it by the skin of his teeth—and at the sacrifice of not stopping for a coffee at Timmy's, or anywhere else. There wasn't even time to buy one in the airport lounge. He had a window seat and hoped he might have the row to himself, but just before the doors closed a short man in a business suit came sliding down the aisle, re-opened the overhead bin to store his own sleek suitcase, seated himself, smiled at Matthew, and stuck out his hand. "Savio," he said. "Savio Malise."

Matthew sighed inwardly, sensing a talkative companion, but he shook the other man's hand. "Matthew Harding."

"Are you on holiday, Mr. Harding?" asked Savio.

"Matthew. Please. Travelling on business, unfortunately." He glanced at Savio's face in profile, and it struck him there was something familiar about him, though he couldn't place where he had seen him before.

"No matter. There's always pleasure to be had," said Savio, almost—but not quite—leering. "What line of business are you in, Matthew?"

"I'm a private investigator," said Matthew reluctantly. Telling people this often led to lousy jokes or lengthy recollections of favourite television shows.

"Well, how interesting," said Savio. "That must be *fascinating* work. Or am I wrong? Do you have to put up with the tedium that afflicts every other profession?"

"It has its share of tedious days," said Matthew.

"Isn't that the human condition?" said Savio. "Take me. I'm in executive recruitment, and you'd think I'd lead a life of interesting conversations with high-powered people, often over fancy dinners. But no."

"It isn't like that?" asked Matthew, intuiting that the question was expected of him.

"Paperwork," said Savio. "I'm buried in paperwork. Dear me, it never ends. So, what sort of investigation takes you to Mexico?"

"It's a missing person's case. But I'm afraid I can say no more about it."

"Then say no more," said Savio, holding up his hand and smiling broadly. "I respect discretion. We have to be very discreet in my business, too. No executive wants his company to know that he's looking at other job opportunities."

"I suppose not," said Matthew.

"You'd suppose correctly," said Savio, mysteriously tapping the side of his nose. "I'm on *discreet* business myself right this instant. I usually operate out of Toronto and London—I mean the UK London, you understand—but this time business calls me to Mexico City."

"A first for you?" asked Matthew.

"Oh, no," said Savio. "I've been there before, and I've no doubt I'll be there again—but it's a little unusual. Not part of the standard routine."

"Ah," said Matthew.

". . . And then I'm off to Oaxaca," said Savio. "But that's a brief vacation."

"Oh, really?" said Matthew. "As it happens, I'm going to Oaxaca, too."

"Well, well," said Savio. "What a happy coincidence! I'm not flying straight down myself—as I say, I have some business to attend to in Mexico City first—but I'll be following you in just a day or two. We might bump into each other while we're there!"

"Well, I suppose we might," said Matthew, "though I gather it's a big state."

"It is, it is!" Savio laughed. "But one never knows!"

At this moment the buckle-up signs came on, and the pre-take off routines commenced. Matthew stared out the window. He'd flown a number of times in his life, but he'd never gotten over the thrill of seeing the land recede below him as the plane ascended. Even knowing the physics of it, it seemed somehow miraculous. "Amazing, isn't it?" said Savio, looking out the window, too—and in that moment Matthew thought that perhaps he'd misjudged the man; perhaps he was simply a friendly soul with a desire to make the flight more pleasant by generating a little human warmth. Perhaps he hadn't 'leered' when talking about the pleasure to be had, even when travelling on business. *I'm such a judgemental son of a bitch*, he thought. *I need to be kinder to strangers.* And so, as the trip unfolded, he did tell Savio a little more about what took him to Mexico, though of course he avoided giving any names. His seat companion listened with close attention and growing gravity, and when Matthew fell asleep a couple of hours later, having eaten a perfectly palatable dinner and drunk a glass of wine, he did so vaguely hoping that he and Mr. Malise might indeed bump into one another in Oaxaca.

★ ★ ★

Matthew awakened reasonably refreshed, though stiff, just as the plane was beginning its descent into Mexico City. The night cityscape was not as brightly lit as a North American city would have been, but he had, even so, a sense of a vast urban centre. He felt an urgent need to urinate, and he worried that his breath would be anything but fresh, but recognized he'd be unable to do anything about either of these things until after the plane landed. Savio, however, seemed to read his mind, for he took a pack of tiny peppermint candies from his pocket and offered them to Matthew.

"Thank you," said Matthew, spilling several into his hand.

"I never travel without them," said Savio. "I spend so much of my time on planes."

"I'll remember that tip," said Matthew, returning the pack.

"Mexico City," said Savio, gazing out the window. "A fascinating place. So much beauty, and so much corruption. So much integrity, and so much violence. But you won't really see anything beyond the terminal."

"Not on this trip, no," said Matthew. "I hope to see something of Oaxaca, though."

"Oaxaca is also fascinating," said Savio. "It too has a violent past, but it's become much more . . . civilized in recent years. It doesn't have the drug wars one sees in the north. You'll be able to walk the streets with confidence, even in the late evening."

"Good," said Matthew.

"You must visit Monte Alban, if you get the chance."

"What is Monte Alban?"

Savio smiled. "It's a wonderful ruined city in the mountains above the Valley of Oaxaca," he said. "The excavation isn't complete, but what they have revealed so far is amazing. And there are such marvellous views of the valley and the surrounding countryside! If you have a few hours free, you must visit."

"If I have, I certainly will," said Matthew, "but I expect to spend the bulk of my time in Huajuapan."

"Huajuapan I don't know at all," said Savio. "Perhaps one day you will tell me what you find there."

"I hope I have the chance,' said Matthew, buckling up his seatbelt as the flight attendant came down the aisle.

CHAPTER FIFTEEN

The Mexico City terminal was large, crowded and surprisingly chilly: the airport authorities apparently kept the air-conditioning cranked up high. Matthew had a four-hour layover, and he spent much of the time just walking about, though he also bought a gratifyingly good sandwich at one of the several restaurants in his wing of the building. The bathrooms, he found, were relatively clean, but the two he visited had run out of paper towels. He pointed this out to the cleaner, but this gentleman simply shrugged: "No más por tres horas," he said—a sentence helpfully translated by a young man wearing a University of Arizona sweat shirt as, "No more for three hours."

The flight to Oaxaca City lasted fifty minutes. The mountains below looked austerely beautiful in the early morning sun. Matthew's seat companions were a brown-skinned mother and her young daughter, who spent much of the journey talking quietly with one another. Matthew guessed they were Mixteco, one of the indigenous peoples of southern Mexico. The little girl smiled at him, and he smiled back, but neither attempted conversation.

Matthew lingered in the arrivals and departures lounge as he checked websites to see where he might stay in the city. He eventually settled on a modestly-priced hotel on the outskirts of Oaxaca, and telephoned to make a reservation. The woman at the other end spoke English proficiently, and his taxi driver took him there for what struck Matthew as a very reasonable fare. Andrew's money would clearly go some distance in Mexico.

At the hotel, Matthew signed in and showed his passport. The desk clerk's English was much more laboured than the telephone receptionist's, but she understood that he wished to speak to the manager, and she showed him into an office on the other side of the lobby. A handsome, well-dressed man rose to greet him. "How may I help you, Señor?"

"I am visiting Oaxaca for several days and want to travel to Huajuapan and, possibly, to other places as well, but I speak very little Spanish. Do you know of a translator I could hire to travel with me? I would pay a good wage."

"First, welcome to Oaxaca," said the manager. "As to your request, I must think a little. Would you give me a few minutes to rake through my brains and make a telephone call?"

Matthew suppressed a smile at *rake through my brains*. "Of course. I'll check into my room and wait to hear from you. I'm in room 106. Matthew Harding."

"By all means check into your room, Mr. Harding," said the manager, "but then go and have a drink by the pool. I will find you there."

"That sounds like a good idea," said Matthew. A bell-hop waited for him, and he followed him out the back door and onto a sidewalk running between the main building and a lush lawn punctuated with flower beds and planted with healthy trees. His room had an ensuite bathroom, an air-conditioner, a television and a queen-size bed: it was small, but it had everything he needed.

Matthew ordered breakfast at the poolside restaurant, then sat and enjoyed the morning sun. With only two hours of sleep under his belt he was tired, but the coffee gave him a boost, and he figured he'd be fully functional until early afternoon—at which point, yes, he'd definitely need a nap. He was contemplating a third cup when the hotel manager appeared on the pool deck with a handsome fellow of about twenty-eight in tow.

"Señor, I present to you Fernando," said the manager. "He has studied at the university and also spent some time in your country. He will be a fine translator for you."

Matthew rose and shook the young man's hand. "A pleasure to meet you, Fernando," he said. And to the hotel manager: "Thank you."

"It's my pleasure, Señor Harding," said the manager, "I will leave you to attend to your business." With a slight bow, he left the two men alone.

Matthew indicated that Fernando should sit. "May I offer you a coffee? Something to eat?"

"I have eaten, thank you," said Fernando, "but a coffee would be nice." His English was every bit as good as the manager's, and he had an easy manner to him that Matthew immediately liked.

Matthew signalled the waiter and pointed at his coffee cup, then at his guest. "How did you come to spend time in Canada?"

"My fiancée lives there," said Fernando. "She is Canadian. We met when she was teaching here in Mexico."

"Are you planning to join her permanently?"

Fernando frowned. "I would like to, but immigrating to Canada is not easy," he said. "They seem to think that Mexicans will end up on welfare."

"And you have a university education?" said Matthew.

"I have an engineering degree," said Fernando, "but maybe there are many engineers in Canada." He shrugged.

Matthew doubted that Canada had a surplus of bilingual engineers, but did not say so. "Your English is very fluent."

"My university required that engineers study English for five years," said Fernando. "It is not enough for fluency, but six months in Ottawa made me much more confident. And my fiancée teaches English."

"Excellent," said Matthew. "To business, if I may. I need a translator for the next few days, and possibly a week, and I will guarantee at least four days at three thousand pesos per day—plus I will of course pay all travel and food costs, and provide a separate hotel room when we travel away from Oaxaca City. Are you interested?"

"You are not in the drug business?" Fernando asked, looking him in the eyes.

"God, no," said Matthew.

"Then, yes," said Fernando. "I will do it."

"You are free?" asked Matthew.

"I will make myself free," said Fernando. "I have a job here, but I can pay someone to cover for me."

Matthew counted out three thousand Mexican pesos. "Here is your first day's pay in advance," he said, "to help with any arrangements you need to make." He handed the notes to Fernando. "Do you know Huajuapan, incidentally?"

"Huajuapan is my home town," said Fernando, grinning broadly. "I went to university there."

"Is it easy to get to by public transport?"

Fernando considered this for a moment. "I think I would recommend that you hire a driver to take you," he said. "The bus is very slow and very crowded, and sometimes there is no air conditioning."

"Okay," said Matthew. "Can you arrange for a car and driver?"

"I can do that," said Fernando, "or you could rent a car and I could drive us. That way we can come and go as you please. And it would be cheaper than hiring a driver. The front desk can order you a car."

"That makes good sense," said Matthew. "I'm going to have a shower, and a nap. Can you be back here at 3:00?"

"Yes," said Fernando. He took a gulp of his coffee, got up, shook Matthew's hand again, and left. Matthew watched him go, then headed off to check out and order a car.

Chapter Sixteen

Matthew read in bed, then fell asleep to the sound of maids chattering cheerfully outside his room. He woke some hours later to the chirping of his phone alarm. When he reached for his cell, he discovered he had a headache. "Shit!" he said, got out of bed, drank half a bottle of water, then went into the bathroom to brush his teeth again, taking the water bottle with him. He contemplated having another shower to help him wake up, but, checking the time, decided against, and began getting dressed and repacking his bag. As he was doing so, his phone rang.

"Do you have any news?" asked Andrew, sounding at once sad and hopeful.

Matthew felt a tug at his heart. "I can tell you that I'm in Mexico, and that I've hired a translator," he said. "We're leaving for Huajuapan very soon."

"I just thought I'd check," said Andrew. "I'm going a little crazy here."

"I understand," said Matthew. "How's your painting coming?"

Andrew's voice brightened a little: "I've made some progress with the nativity scene," he said, "but I've also decided to do a whole series of pictures illustrating New Testament stories. Or, at least, those that Edwin Long didn't get around to painting."

"So what's next?" asked Matthew.

"I thought I'd begin with a painting of Jesus being baptized in the river Jordan," said Andrew. "Lots of painters have done that one, but Long didn't. I've already sketched in the figures."

"Would you send me a photo of it?"

"Sure," said Andrew, though he sounded surprised. "If you really want, I'll take a picture right now and send it to you. But it's just a sketch—there's no colour."

"I'd really like to see it," said Matthew. "I'm interested in all kinds of religious art, and I admire your work."

"It's in front of me right now," said Andrew. "I'll send you a picture as soon as I hang up."

Two minutes later Matthew had an image on his screen.

Andrew had told the truth: the image was simply a sketch. It showed, in the foreground, a bearded man, rather wild in appearance, standing tall in a river, tenderly cradling the head of another man, also bearded, in the water. Several things immediately struck Matthew: first, the raw, feral power of the man standing, and the comparative passivity, in the moment, of the man whose head had just been lifted above the water's surface. Second, the fact that, in spite of his apparent power, the baptizer was looking at the other with a kind of reverence. Third, that the man being baptized—surely Jesus—was looking towards the sky with an expression of poignant sadness. It was astonishing what emotion Andrew had been able to convey with a few lines. A small crowd was gathered on the bank, all, with one exception, watching the baptizer and the baptized, but one, a woman, looking sharply to her left, further downstream, as though she had just seen or heard something. The image on the phone was, of course, very small— much smaller than the picture Andrew had sketched—but even so Matthew found himself fascinated by it. When he closed his eyes, he still saw the figures clearly, as though they had been somehow seared onto the inside of his eyelids. *Andrew's talented*, he thought. *The guy is really talented.*

Matthew did a last check of his room, then, with twenty minutes to go before Fernando would be returning, he went out once again to the pool area, where he ordered his third cup of coffee. The pool deck was busier now: a Mexican family with a mother, father, grandmother and three children were all there. The adults were sitting in deck chairs, while the children frolicked in the pool. One of the little girls tripped and fell climbing out of the pool, and when she began crying her father got up, scooped her into his arms, kissed the top of her head, and delivered her to her mother, who spent the next few moments rocking and soothing her until she relaxed and laughed at the antics of her slightly older brother and sister. Her brother brought her a rubber ball, and she threw it for him to fetch from the pool, the boy pretending to be a retriever. Matthew was charmed by this—but it also awakened in him an old sadness, the sadness of a man who had desperately wanted children and a full family life, but who had lost the chance when his wife's struggles with cancer began in her late twenties. Grace. *Grace.*

Fernando came out onto the pool deck, smiling. "Hola," he said, "the car is out front."

"Hello, again," said Matthew. "Let's go." The car was a mid-sized Ford, the gas tank was full, and Matthew was beginning to feel a sense of control and confidence when he saw in the side mirror a young man in blue jeans and a ball cap emerge from the hotel and watch them go. He was carrying a skateboard. Matthew made an involuntary sound in his throat.

"Is something wrong?" Fernando asked.

"No," said Matthew. "Just a kid with a skateboard."

"The roads are not good for skateboarding here," said Fernando, negotiating the car around a milk carton lying in the street. "Maybe he is going to one of the skate parks."

Maybe, Matthew thought.

Chapter Seventeen

So long as they were in Oaxaca City, Matthew stayed awake. He watched the streetscape pass with interest, noting that expensive car dealerships stood cheek-by-jowl with shops selling cheap furniture and household goods. Similarly, some of the residences were built with care and expertise, while others were scarcely more than shacks. They passed several stately churches, and many scrapyards. Oaxaca was, in that tired old phrase, a city of contrasts. Just as interesting, to Matthew, were the mountains in the background—but the background eventually became foreground, and he saw that they were ascending. "Huajuapan is in the mountains?" he asked Fernando.

"Yes," said Fernando. "You will find the drive interesting."

But Matthew had still not fully recovered from flying overnight, and he drifted into sleep as Fernando drove them higher into the mountains. As he tried to keep his eyes open, he had impressions, every now and then, of an arid landscape. His knowledge of trees was not great, but he thought he recognized pine and oak straggling up the mountain slopes—though there were also many rock-faces and outcrops. They saw a number of cars heading toward Oaxaca City: some of them were as modern as their own, but others looked positively ancient, possibly held together with twine, chicken-wire and chewing gum.

But when Matthew fell fully asleep, that dry and mountainous landscape disappeared. In his dream the time of day was much the same as the time of day in Oaxaca, but the light was filtered through leaves, a little softer. He was walking through a landscape of almond, chestnut and olive trees, and he could hear, over the rise of a small hill, the sound of water flowing. As he walked on, he could also hear, more and more plainly, a strong voice crying out, *Nacham! Nacham!* . . . and every now and then he thought he heard snatches of a flute.

He was getting closer and closer to the top of the hill, when his friendly seat-companion from the Mexico City flight appeared from behind a tree in front of him. "Matthew!" Savio called out, beaming and spreading his arms as if to offer a hug. "How wonderful to see you!"

"It's good to see you, too, Savio," said Matthew. "But what brings you here?"

"Well, I have something to show you!" said Savio. "I mean, honestly, I didn't know you were coming, but I cannot think of anyone I'd rather share this with!"

"Is it over the hill?" Matthew asked.

"Over the hill?" said Savio. "No, no—it's this way." And he pointed toward a dense clump of what looked like fig trees to his left. "Come and see!"

Matthew was puzzled in his turn, because the call from the river—if a river was indeed the source of the watery sounds—was welcoming, but he followed his friend into the grove of figs. "So, you see," said Savio—

But in that instant Matthew heard two distinct thuds as if two people had jumped from the trees behind him; he felt a terrible blow to the head, and as he lay on the ground, a crushing kick to his ribs—

"Matthew! Matthew!" Fernando was shaking him. Matthew was back in the car, and Fernando was shaking him awake as he pulled to the side of the road. "Are you all right?"

"God," said Matthew. "That was a vivid dream."

"More like a nightmare," said Fernando. "A daytime nightmare. You were shouting."

"It's okay, I'm back," said Matthew. "But, yes, it was a real nightmare." He gingerly felt the back of his head, and winced as his fingers probed a gathering bruise. He coughed—and clutched his side. "Jesus!" he said.

"Are you in pain?" asked Fernando.

"Just a stitch in my side," said Matthew. "Strange."

"It is not your heart?"

"No. No, I'm confident it's not my heart. Don't worry, Fernando."

Fernando looked at him with real concern for a moment, then nodded. He glanced at his rear-view mirror, signalled, and pulled off the shoulder and back onto the road. "Day-time dreams can be very realistic," he said. "You don't fall completely asleep, maybe, and your brain is spinning."

They drove in silence for a while, Fernando focused on the road, and Matthew massaging his ribs and marvelling at how suggestible his conscious mind was to dreams. "How much farther?" he asked.

"Another hour," said Fernando. "We have made good time."

"This is all very familiar to you? The sights?"

"Yes," said Fernando. "I didn't often travel to Oaxaca when I was a boy, but my village is also in the mountains and it is like this." He gestured in a way that took in everything they saw. "It is . . . *dramatic*, I think is the word you would use."

"Dramatic is a good word," said Matthew. And you went to school in Huajuapan?"

"I went to high school and university there," said Fernando. "UTM—the Technological University of the Mixteca. It is still quite new."

"Is it an expensive school?"

"So long as you keep up your grades the state pays," said Fernando. "I worked very hard." He smiled. "Where are we going first?"

Matthew showed a slip of paper to Fernando. "Here," he said. "The Garcia Peral."

Fernando glanced at the paper. "I know it," he said. "A good place."

"We'll go there," said Matthew, "grab some dinner, then— well, we'll see. I don't know whether we'll be able to do anything tonight, or if we'll have to wait until the morning."

They were now on a particularly winding section of the highway where seeing ahead was complicated by the fact that the road was carved out of the face of the mountain. Fernando had slowed their speed and had both hands on the wheel. "This is where my grandmother closes her eyes," he said. "Just for the next few minutes."

"Oh, I trust you," said Matthew. At that instant a large and overloaded logging truck came around the bend immediately in front of them. It was going too fast, and just for a second, as the driver jerked the wheel to get out of Fernando's lane, it looked as though the truck might tip—

"*Idiota!*" said Fernando, jerking his own wheel to the right and toward the face of the mountain. The logging truck righted itself, but not before a single log dislodged from the rest of the load and rolled over the side, tumbling to the tarmac only yards behind them as the truck whipped past.

"Good Christ!" said Matthew. "Should we go back and see if there's anything we can do?"

"It's not safe to turn around here," said Fernando. "There's a restaurant coming up. We can stop there and report it to the highway patrol."

"I can use my cell," said Matthew. As he reached into his pocket, he was surprised to feel it buzzing. There was a text waiting for him. From an unknown number. "Maybe next time." He felt a chill at the base of his spine.

CHAPTER EIGHTEEN

The hotel was attractive—more upscale than the place Matthew had stayed in Oaxaca. The gentleman at the front desk spoke decent English, and they were attended to quickly. After checking in, Matthew asked to speak to the manager.

"Is there a problem, Señor?" asked the desk clerk.

"Not at all," said Matthew. "Go ahead to your room, Fernando," he added. "Let's meet in the restaurant for coffee in twenty minutes."

The hotel manager introduced himself and invited Matthew into his office. "How may I help you?" he asked.

"I'd like to show you a brief video," said Matthew. "It was taken here in Huajuapan, but I don't know where. I'm hoping you may be able to identify the facility."

"The facility?" asked the manager.

"Uh, the hall—the place where the people are gathered. It's a wedding."

"The *instalaciones*," said the manager. "If it is not in a church, I should be able to tell you easily. I know all the wedding *instalaciones*."

"That's what I hoped," said Matthew, and he clicked on the wedding video and handed his phone to the manager.

The manager watched the video for a few seconds, then pressed pause. "You won't have far to go, Señor," he said. "It is across the road from us now. You walk out the front door and there it is."

"That's a stroke of good luck, then," said Matthew. "I don't suppose you recognize anyone in the video?"

The manager clicked play and watched to the end. "No, Señor," he said. "I thought maybe one of the bridesmaids . . . but no. They may be from one of the villages outside Huajuapan. Or they may be from different *círculos* than those I move in. Huajuapan is not big, but we all have our own small . . ."

"Circles," said Matthew.

"Sí. Circles. And most of the people who stay here are not from here."

"The white woman—you don't remember her from a few weeks ago?"

"She might have stayed here, Señor," he said, "but we have many, many guests. She is beautiful, but no. I don't remember her."

"I appreciate your help," said Matthew, taking back his phone. "Do you think the facility will be open this late?"

"I am sure the owner will be there," said the manager. "This is a busy season for them, and there are weddings every weekend."

"Thank you for your time, sir," said Matthew, getting up.

"Enjoy your stay with us," said the manager. "We get many visitors, but not many from Canada."

Matthew unpacked his shirts, underwear and toiletries, then checked his email. There was a message from Sharon: *Matthew, are you okay? I got a scary call from someone with a guttural voice. He wasn't speaking English, but I heard him say your name a couple of times. TBH I'm really weirded out about it.*

Matthew closed his eyes and thought for a moment: more strangeness. *I'm fine*, he wrote back. *Don't worry about me. But if you're spooked, feel free to take tomorrow off. Just put a sign on the door.* He hoped Sharon would check her messages that evening.

Matthew and Fernando bumped into each other on the stairs. "We're going across the street to a kind of banquet hall," Matthew said. "I may need your translating skills. We'll get a coffee with dinner later."

"I'm ready," said Fernando. "I've never seen this place."

They entered a lobby that opened up into a large hall. It had a stone floor and a high ceiling, and looked as though it could accommodate two hundred people. A team of six men and women were clearing away tables and chairs from what had been a dining set-up. As they went into the hall itself, an older man detached himself from the other workers and greeted them in Spanish.

Fernando replied, then turned to Matthew. "He is asking if we want to rent the hall."

"Please tell him no," said Matthew, "but ask if I can show him a one-minute video. I want to know if he recognizes the people in it."

Fernando passed this on to the older man who shrugged, then signaled his assent. Matthew handed over his cell phone. When the gentleman hesitated, Fernando leaned forward and pressed play. The gentleman watched to the end, looked up, and spoke briefly. Fernando translated: "He says it's the Flores wedding, a few weeks ago. A nice wedding. He wants to know what this is about."

"Can you tell him I'm a private investigator looking for the young white woman at the end of the video?"

Fernando passed this on. The gentleman said something, and Fernando responded. "He asks if *private investigator* is the same as police. I told him no."

The gentleman spoke again, at some length. Fernando heard him out, then: "He says he remembers the white girl, but did not speak to her. The bride is from a village outside town, almost a local, but the groom, Pedro Flores, is from Oaxaca City. He gives tours at Monte Alban, and he and his bride have an apartment there—that's where he sent the bill for the wedding. It has been paid. There is no problem."

Matthew nodded. "Can you ask him if he recognizes the man sitting beside the white woman?"

Fernando put the question, then showed the man where to press replay. He watched again, then spoke.

"No," says Fernando. "He thinks he has seen him before, but he doesn't know where. He didn't make any trouble with the waitresses or the band. He had no reason to take notice of him. The girl was easier to remember. I think he says this as a little joke, man to man."

Matthew forced himself to give a chuckle. "Thank him for me, would you, Fernando? And tell him he has a nice place here."

Fernando did this, then he and Matthew shook hands with the banquet hall owner. As they left, someone unseen switched on the sound system, and the Rolling Stones' "Sympathy for the Devil" blared out of six large speakers.

CHAPTER NINETEEN

"Where shall we eat?" asked Matthew, as they stepped back out onto the street.

"What kind of food do you want?" asked Fernando.

"I want to eat what people here eat," said Matthew. "I'm not big on spices, but I'll try most things once."

"There's a *taqueria* not far from here where ordinary Mexicans like to go. The food is good, and it's cheap."

"You've sold me," said Matthew. "Lead the way."

They made their way to the end of their little street, then turned left onto another, this one fronting a plaza. There were small-scale carousel rides and a bouncy castle for children on the other side, and food kiosks lining the plaza side of the street. In the distance, and through the branches of a number of trees, Matthew could see two spires of what he guessed was a large church. "This is the Antonio de Leon central plaza," said Fernando. "And next door is the Cathedral of Our Lady of Guadalupe." He had to speak loudly to make himself heard above the music blaring from the rides.

"If we have some free time, I'd like to visit the cathedral," Matthew said. He waved at a child who was pointing out the big white man to his mother.

"It was damaged in an earthquake. You can't go inside," said Fernando. "We turn here." The narrow sidewalks were full of people, but no one hindered their passage. Some clearly shared the child's curiosity about Matthew, but it seemed a friendly curiosity—and most were indifferent. A vendor tried to sell them a bag of peanuts, but did not persist when he saw they were not interested. An old woman was seated on the pavement outside a food store begging for change, and Matthew stooped and put twenty pesos in her outstretched hands. In a couple of minutes they were climbing a flight of indoor stairs that led to a crowded, noisy and hot dining area. "The Taqueria El Chumbia," said Fernando. "It's always busy."

They were seated quickly, and Fernando advised Matthew on what he should order. Their tacos arrived moments later, and they both tucked in happily, drinking *agua de melon*, made from water, cantaloupe and a little sugar, with their meal. "This is good," said Matthew.

"We will make a Mexican of you," said Fernando, raising his glass.

Choosing to trust Fernando, Matthew took the opportunity of the meal to explain what he was doing in Huajuapan. He showed Fernando the video, and told him about Andrew and about the rogue wave that had apparently knocked Hannah off the whale-watching boat. His companion listened carefully, not speaking until Matthew had finished. "Do you have a theory for what happened?" Fernando asked.

"Not yet," said Matthew. "I have suspicions . . . but no theory."

"Do you often have bad dreams?" Fernando asked. He had put down his glass and was looking at Matthew intently.

Matthew was taken aback by the question. "I have had some very vivid dreams recently," he replied. "But why do you ask?"

"Have you had those dreams since you took on this case?"

Matthew thought for a moment. "Yes. But how is that relevant?"

"I am Mixtec," said Fernando. "I've had a modern education, and I've travelled, but I was brought up in a small village, and I remember the things my grandparents taught me."

"About dreams?" asked Matthew.

"About many things," said Fernando, "but, yes, about dreams, too. They believe that sometimes the spirit leaves the body when we sleep—that it goes to places and times the body cannot visit." He looked around the room. "They taught me that what we see when we are awake is not the only reality."

"There's a sense in which I believe that," said Matthew. "I'm a quietly religious man. I don't talk about it, but I read a lot, and I like sacred art and music and architecture. I don't give much weight to dreams, though. I've always seen them as epiphenomena."

"Epiphenomena?" said Fernando.

"A mental state that's a by-product of brain activity. The brain randomly releasing chemicals as it rests."

"But your dreams are coherent? Fernando asked.

"Sometimes."

"Recently?"

"Yes," Matthew admitted. "Recently they've followed a kind of plot-line with recurring characters."

"So not so random," said Fernando.

"No. Not completely random."

"Well . . ." said Fernando, and he allowed his voice to trail off.

At that instant Matthew noticed that four tough-looking young men at a table over by one wall were watching him and Fernando. The two facing away from him had twisted their heads and bodies around to look. "We're being scrutinized," he told Fernando.

Fernando turned his head and took in the group of young men. "They're probably just curious," he said, "but if you're uncomfortable, we can go."

"Yeah, let's go," said Matthew. "I'll pay the bill, then let's take a walk. We should head back to Oaxaca City early tomorrow morning."

"Do you mind if I visit with some friends later this evening?" Fernando asked. "I don't often get back home."

"No problem," said Matthew. "Just point me in the direction of the hotel, and I'll be fine. I'll pick up a map there, and explore a little on foot."

"You shouldn't walk around town without an escort," said Fernando. "We'll walk together. I can see my friends later. I'll just text them quickly." He fired off a quick message.

"Okay. I just want to stretch my legs for half an hour," said Matthew. He placed some bills on the table. "Let's go," he said.

The four young men got up too, and followed Matthew and Fernando toward the stairs. Matthew noticed that Fernando's shoulders had tightened.

CHAPTER TWENTY

The streets were even busier than they had been forty minutes earlier, and for a moment or two Matthew thought that he and Fernando would have no difficulty putting some distance between themselves and the four young men—if they were in fact being followed. But he had reckoned without the drawback of his own height, and the determination of their pursuers. It was swiftly evident that they *were* being followed. "Should we look for the police?" Matthew asked.

"No," said Fernando, glancing back.

"Why not?"

"Mexican police are not like your police in Canada," said Fernando. He quickened his pace a little, taking them away from the direction in which they had come.

Matthew was suddenly concerned that he had misread Fernando—that his young translator might be leading him into a trap. "Why are we going away from the hotel?" he asked.

"Because my friends are coming to meet us from this direction," said Fernando.

"The friends you texted?" said Matthew.

"Yes," said Fernando. "They are close now. Turn here." They turned into a side street where there were considerably fewer people, and Fernando broke into a jog. Matthew cursed, then followed suit. Glancing back, he saw the four thugs—the word seemed apt—turn the corner and immediately break into a run. Fernando had his cell up to his ear and he said something sharp—and a few seconds later two figures stepped out from an alley-way a half block in front of them. "My friends," said Fernando, slowing. The friends called out something and began to run towards them. Fernando and Matthew stopped and turned to face their pursuers, who pulled up abruptly. There was a pause, a pregnant silence, then one of them took a single step forward and said something in a language that was neither Spanish nor English. Fernando replied, and at that instant his two friends came up and stood flanking them. The two groups stood staring at each other.

"A Mexican stand-off," said Matthew, under his breath.

"They are cowards," said Fernando quietly. "Four on two they liked. Four on four, not so much." Matthew had not liked running. Part of him hoped there would be violence, a kind of catharsis. He felt an itch in his fists. He stretched his hands and wriggled his fingers before clenching them again.

The leader of the four pursuers spoke again, saying something clearly intended to be threatening—then spat on the street. Neither Fernando nor his friends replied: they held their ground. There was a long pause, then the pack leader turned and headed back up the street they'd come down, his three henchmen in his wake. Matthew saw the body language of his own companions relax a little. When the pursuers turned the corner and vanished from sight, Fernando and his friends collectively released their breath.

"Good," said Fernando. "Good. Matthew, this is Carlos and Hugo. We have two other friends coming, too, but they are still a little distance away." He gave each of his friends a warm hug, and patted them on their backs.

Matthew shook their hands. "*Gracias*—thank you," he said. "And Fernando, what language were those men speaking?"

"Zapotec," said the friend called Hugo.

"You speak English?" said Matthew.

"A little," said Hugo. "I was at the university with Fer."

"And you, Carlos?" said Matthew, turning to the other fellow. Carlos smiled and shook his head.

"Carlos did not go to the university," said Fernando. "He is my cousin, and an old friend of mine. We grew up together. He and Hugo are more like brothers to me."

"Is this common, Fer?" asked Matthew, picking up on Fernando's nickname. "This chasing after foreigners—menacing people in the streets."

"No—" said Fernando and Hugo at the same time. "It is very unusual," Fernando added. "The police are not good, but they get upset when foreigners are attacked. It brings attention."

"It brings the newspapers and the *Federales*," said Hugo. "Not good. I am shaking a little." He held out his hands, palms down, and laughed.

"Let me buy you all a beer," said Matthew.

"How about we walk for a little bit, then go back to our hotel and have beers there?" said Fernando. "Oh, here are Edel and Gio." Two other young men had emerged from the alley-way, and Fernando embraced them before introducing them to Matthew.

The six men spent the next half hour walking the streets of Huajuapan, the Mexicans laughing at shared memories and jokes, while Matthew drank in the sights of a town unlike anywhere he'd been before, with its mostly narrow streets and sidewalks, its low-rise buildings, and its startling (to his eyes) blend of indigenous, country folk—many of them quite short—and a more sleek and prosperous-looking class, still short, but taller, certainly, than their country cousins. He was aware, though, that no matter how much Fernando laughed and joked with his friends, he was also keeping his eyes wide open, and Matthew realized that the universe had been kind in sending him this particular translator.

Nearly to the minute of the half hour, Matthew saw that Fernando had steered them back to the street with the banquet hall and their own hotel. He led the way in, then ushered the others into the restaurant, where they took a table and ordered nachos and beer. And there they spent the next hour or so, before Matthew, recognizing that he might be dampening the general mirth with his need for regular translation, announced that he was going to bed early. He paid the bill, arranged to meet Fernando at breakfast, shook hands all round, then went back to the desk in the lobby to collect his room key. But as he was turning away from the desk, he noticed a collection of luggage off to one side, and there, among the bags and suitcases, a skateboard with a fading Toronto Raptors sticker on its deck.

CHAPTER TWENTY-ONE

Matthew stared at the skateboard. He had a good visual memory, and this skateboard was either similar, or identical, to the one wielded by the teenager at the bus stop back in Toronto. He did not remember the Raptors sticker—and that might mean that this wasn't the same skateboard—but, on the other hand, the day of the attack had been punctuated by a car accident that took place under his nose, so it was excusable if some details had eluded him then, or slipped away from him since. *But what are you thinking?* he asked himself. *Of* course *this isn't the same skateboard.* Of course that particular idiot hadn't followed him all the way from Toronto, via Mexico City and Oaxaca. It was impossible.

Acting on impulse he turned back to the fellow on duty at the desk. "Excuse me," he said, "but are these things going to be taken upstairs?"

"No, Señor," said the desk clerk. "The guests checked out. They go out to dinner somewhere. They leave hotel tonight. We keep luggage for them for taxi, for airport."

"Ah, okay," said Matthew. He contemplated sitting on the couch and waiting for the diners to return, but he found himself tired. *I'm getting old*, he thought. *Too many stressors in my life. Since when did I want my bed at 8:30 p.m.?* He climbed the stairs to his room.

He showered, and lay down on the bed staring at the ceiling. In the last sixty-something hours, he realized, he'd been nearly hit by a car . . . and seen a man die in front of his eyes; he'd been assaulted with a skateboard; he'd been nearly crushed under a log tumbling from a logging truck; and he'd been chased by four Zapotec thugs with violence on their minds. And it's not as if his sleep had been restful, either. He could not remember ever having had such vivid dreams. He found himself wishing, urgently, that he had someone he could talk to—someone who knew him well. A vivid image of Grace—brown eyes open, gazing up at him from her hospital bed—bloomed in his mind . . . and just as suddenly disappeared. *She's gone, Matthew*, he thought. *She's gone. Let her go.*

Sharon. Of course. Sharon. It was not too late to call. He punched in her number, and she answered almost immediately. "Hello, Matt!" Her voice was warm.

"How are you?" he asked.

"Much better," she said. "I went to a yoga class after work, then came home and had a glass of wine with dinner. I got a little perspective on things. How are *you*?"

"I'm fine," said Matthew, deciding in that instant that he would not burden Sharon with the strange experiences he was having. "Mexico is an interesting country. I wish I could explore it as a tourist."

"I don't believe you," Sharon said—but she said it lightly. "You'd be bored out of your mind without a mission of some kind."

"I'm not so sure," said Matthew. "I'm beginning to see the attraction of swimming pools and tall, cold drinks."

"Now you're speaking my language," said Sharon. "As long as there's a good book at my elbow."

"This voice on the phone," said Matthew. "Have you any sense what language he was speaking?"

"No, and I've decided it was a crank call," said Sharon. "He was probably saying that you had a computer virus and that you need to grant him access to delete it for you. Just some sort of scam. We get two or three of those a week. It's just that this one was in Klingon."

Matthew laughed. "So long as you're not weirded out any longer. But do feel free to take tomorrow off."

"I'm a big girl," said Sharon. "I'll be at my desk. I have an essay to write in between the *hundreds* of telephone calls I have to attend to. God, you keep me busy, Matt."

"Okay, then," said Matthew. He thought for a moment. "Take care."

"You, too, Matt," said Sharon. "And thanks for calling. It's good to hear your voice."

Matthew hung up, and lay on the bed thinking about Sharon. He felt lucky to have her in his corner. She was a no-drama kind of girl. No, he probably shouldn't think of her as a *girl*. She was a no-drama kind of *woman*. Smart. Beautiful, yes. Warm.

He fell asleep and into a new dream. In it, he was wandering in a stark and barren landscape, almost desert-like—though filled not with sand dunes but with canyons, rock outcroppings and valleys. There was no human in sight, and he had the sense that he could walk for miles, stumbling occasionally on loose pebbles, growing ever thirstier, without seeing anyone. The landscape was not altogether devoid of life, however: he looked down to see a scorpion, yellow, striped, about two-and-a-half inches long, its stinger raised above its back, crossing his path. And then—and, yes, he was surprised—he did see a figure, a white male, tall, straight-backed, and dressed in a business suit, about fifty yards in front of him. He was gazing down into a crater, apparently oblivious of Matthew's approach. Matthew was just about to call out to him when, in the waking world of his hotel room, his cell phone buzzed. There was a text message from the same unidentified number that had sent the "Maybe next time" message. This time it read, "Not quite yet."

Chapter Twenty-Two

Matthew and Fernando left Huajuapan at 9:00 the next morning. It was pouring rain, and Fernando turned the windshield wipers on full as they negotiated their way through the busy, narrow streets and back towards the highway.

"Your friends seem a nice bunch," said Matthew.

"A nice bunch?" Fernando repeated.

"Friendly. Good company."

"We are close," said Fernando. "I wish I could see them more often." There was a large truck ahead of them spewing diesel fumes, and he was keeping far enough behind to avoid their having to breathe them in.

"Let's go directly to Monte Alban and see if Pedro Flores is working today," said Matthew. "I'll worry about finding a place to stay later."

"You can stay with me, if you like," said Fernando. "I share a small apartment, but there is a couch."

"Thank you," said Matthew, "but I won't put you out like that. Your hotels are not expensive here." He was worried that he might cry out in his sleep: the intensity of his dreams was troubling him. And thinking about that caused him to see again the tall male in the business suit who had been in his dream the previous night. Matthew had not seen his face, but for reasons he did not understand, that figure, that presence, unthreatening enough in the description, familiar and yet somehow alien, haunted him. He shook his head to dislodge it.

"Are you okay?" asked Fernando.

"Yes. Yes, I am," said Matthew. "Tell me about Monte Alban."

Fernando smiled. "You would be better off going to Google," he said. But then, growing serious: "It's an ancient

Zapotec city in the mountains, close to Oaxaca City. It was built maybe twenty-five hundred years ago. The engineering is impressive—especially when you think that the building was done without modern machinery."

"It was built by the Zapotec?" said Matthew.

"Mostly. The Olmecs probably put up the first buildings, and the Mixtec took it over from the Zapotec at some point, and then maybe the Aztec before the Spanish arrived. Our peoples were always warring with one another."

"Just like Europe," said Matthew.

"Just like Europe," Fernando agreed. The diesel fume-spewing truck had pulled over, and he swerved to go around it.

Matthew stayed awake for the rest of the journey. He had not travelled much in mountains before this, and he found himself a little dizzy as they rounded some curves. He eventually had the sense that they were descending, and the scenery leveled out somewhat. They began to see some cultivated land, and passed through a couple of villages.

"Did you enjoy your time at university?" Matthew asked.

"It was hard work," said Fernando. "We were not allowed to miss any classes, and we were not allowed to gather with friends on campus. It was very different from the way you do things in Canada."

"You weren't allowed to gather with friends?" Matthew was startled.

"The government was worried about political activism," said Fernando. "But it was a kind of social contract. You didn't pay tuition, but you didn't skip class and you couldn't do politics. The government is trying to create an educated middle-class in one generation. I didn't like it, but I accepted the deal."

"Is it working?" Matthew asked.

"It's too early to say," said Fernando. "I hope it will."

★ ★ ★

They arrived at Monte Alban shortly before noon, and already the day was hot. The rain had stopped, however, and the sky had turned a brilliant blue. To reach the site they had had to go up again, so they were once more in the mountains. They climbed out of the car, passed by several people selling sun hats and handicrafts, bought tickets from a booth just above the parking lot, then immediately went off in search of a public bathroom. They returned to the area around the booth, where a fair number of people were offering their services as tour guides.

"We don't know whether he's an official guide, do we?" Matthew said.

"We don't *know*, but I think he would be," said Fernando. "If you don't have official credentials, you'd have a hard time making a living here. The police would send you away."

"How should we go about this?"

At that moment, a middle-aged woman wearing a badge approached them. "Would you like a tour?" she asked.

"Yes," said Matthew, "but we were hoping we might get one from the friend of a friend. Do you know a Pedro Flores? Is he working today?"

"I know Pedro," said the woman. "He took a large group at around nine, so he will be back soon. But he may want to have something to eat before he takes you."

"That's fine," said Matthew. "But I'd like to book him in advance."

"He will come back there to check in with Mariela," said the woman, pointing to a pretty younger woman standing not far from the ticket booth. "If he wants to rest, and you want to start earlier, I will be happy to take you, if I am not engaged."

"*Gracias*," said Matthew. The woman nodded and moved on.

Fernando cocked his head and looked at Matthew sideways. "You are good with a lie," he said.

"Just for little things," said Matthew, a bit defensively.

"I understand," said Fernando. "There are some things people do not need to know."

Matthew bought a couple of bottles of water while Fernando kept watch, and the two then stood and drank while waiting to see who checked in with Mariela. They saw several guides, male and female, come by and exchange greetings with her, but Fernando suddenly came to attention. "Señor Flores," he said.

It *was* Pedro Flores, and Matthew and Fernando headed towards him as soon as he'd spoken with Mariela. "Mr. Flores," called Matthew.

"Yes?" Pedro turned, and looked a little alarmed as Fernando and Matthew came up to him. It occurred to Matthew suddenly that he might mistake them for undercover policemen.

"My name is Matthew Harding, and this is my friend Fernando Martinez. Could we engage your services?"

"Of course," said Pedro. "But would you excuse me for five minutes?"

"Certainly," said Matthew. Pedro headed off to the bathroom, and returned a couple of minutes later taking a thermos out of his bag.

"Do you mind if I drink while we are walking?" he asked.

"Not at all," said Matthew, opening his wallet and handing Pedro 500 pesos. "But we only need a few minutes of your time."

"It will take longer than that, Señor," said Pedro. "Two hours at least."

"Truthfully, I just want to ask you a few questions," said Matthew, "and then you are free to give another tour." He took out his phone. "I'd like to show you a video shot at your wedding—"

"At my wedding!" Pedro looked from Matthew to Fernando with some alarm.

". . . at your wedding. It was posted to YouTube. I want to ask you to identify a couple of people for us."

"This feels strange," said Pedro, but he pocketed the money. Matthew pressed play, and the young man watched the video.

"It's the two people at the end," said Matthew, "the white woman and the man she is with. What are their names?"

There was a pause, then Pedro began to speak—but he spoke in Spanish, addressing himself to Fernando.

"He says he is not comfortable," said Fernando, "but he will tell you what he knows. He says that these people were there, but they were not invited guests."

"Hang on," said Matthew. "They crashed the wedding?"

"This is not unusual in Oaxaca," Fernando said. He said something soothing to Pedro before turning back to Matthew. "Often, in villages and small towns, people just show up to weddings. The family expects it and makes sure there is enough food and drink for more than they invited. It is a community celebration." He turned back to Pedro and asked something, to which Pedro replied. "He says that he assumed that his bride knew these people, and she assumed that *he* knew them. They were both surprised to see a white woman there." Pedro said something else, gesturing in a way that suggested he was talking about somewhere far away. "He says that one of his cousins spoke to the man during the evening, and he said that he and his girlfriend were going to England, to a place called Salisbury, to work on some sort of archeological . . . digging. That is all he knows, he said."

"Salisbury," said Matthew. "Where the cathedral is?" Fernando spoke to Pedro, and Pedro replied. "He says where there is the place of the standing-stones. Stonehenge. That city."

"Well, well," said Matthew. "Thank him for me, Fernando. Thank you," he added, remembering that of course Pedro spoke some English.

Pedro spoke again. "He asks, can he go now?" said Fernando. "He repeats, this is all he knows."

"This is a good thing you have done, Mr. Flores," said Matthew. "The woman is missing. Her family is upset. You have done them a kindness." Pedro nodded, but he did not look convinced. He looked at Fernando, as if seeking confirmation that he was released, then he left them, disappearing into the crowd of tourists.

"I regret having scared him," said Matthew.

"I don't think *you* scared him," said Fernando. "I think there is something else going on here."

CHAPTER TWENTY-THREE

"What will you do now?" Fernando asked.

"I'm not sure," said Matthew. It may be that I've learned everything I can learn here. If Pedro was telling the truth, I think I need to go to England. Do *you* think he was?"

Fernando thought for a moment. "I think he said what he *believes* to be true," he said finally. "But the video man may have lied to Pedro's cousin."

"I know," said Matthew. "That's my dilemma. They could have stayed in Huajuapan. They could be right here in Oaxaca City. They could be in—I don't know—Hogshollow, Alabama. But I think I have to go to Salisbury."

"*Is* there a Hogshollow in Alabama?" asked Fernando.

"I've no idea," said Matthew. "But while we're here I'd like to look around this place. How do you feel about exploring for a couple of hours?"

"I'm happy to see it again,' said Fernando." I cannot give you a proper tour, but I can tell you what I remember."

"Excellent," said Matthew.

The two set out together, climbing first a small set of stairs, then ascending a slope, then passing under huge laurel trees. There was a choice of paths at this point, one apparently leading to their destination in a relatively gentle but roundabout fashion, while the other required climbing a steep set of steps. They opted for the steps, traversed a grassy verge for a time, then discovered that they had reached the lip of a hill looking down on a vast central plaza. The plaza had buildings ranged around its perimeter, and there were also four large structures in its centre. Matthew was rendered almost speechless by the scale of the place: it was, in fact, a city—a city built two-and-a-half millennia ago, carved out of a mountain top, filled with carefully-engineered buildings, all accomplished, apparently, with hand-tools and human sweat. "I had no idea," he said to Fernando. "No idea at all."

Fernando nodded. "They were violent," he said, "but they weren't primitive."

They went down another set of stairs and entered the central plaza, this new vantage point allowing them to understand the scale of the achievement from another angle. Matthew tried to imagine the place bustling with people, and was not surprised when Fernando told him that at its peak the complex probably accommodated twenty-five thousand people. "This was a political and ceremonial centre," said Fernando. "It was like Mexico City now, or Washington, or London."

"Or Ottawa," said Matthew with a smile.

But Fernando took him seriously. "Yes, like Ottawa," he said, "but an Ottawa where the churches were important. The priests here were very powerful. We think that this was a centre for rituals—that the rituals were why it was built in the first place."

"Well," said Matthew, "there's still a strong ritual aspect to many of the things we do in modern societies."

They walked around the plaza, reading the explanatory panels on some of the buildings, then climbing another flight of steps to reach the highest point on the site, gaining, in the process the best view they'd had yet on the plaza, and, looking the other way, of the Oaxaca Valley below. "They must have felt they were kings of the world up here," said Matthew. They spent some twenty minutes on this level, then decided to go back down. In the back of his mind Matthew was wrestling with whether to fly out that very day, if he could, or stay one night and fly in the morning, but he had been unable to get a wireless signal to check flight schedules. "I'm glad to have seen this," he said, "but I'm feeling guilty about being here if Hannah is in England somewhere."

They descended the steps and were heading across the plaza when they were arrested by a cheerful shout. "Matthew! Matthew, my friend!" Astonished, Matthew and Fernando turned towards the voice, and there was Savio Malise hastening towards them with hand outstretched. "Matthew, what an absolute joy to run into you here!" said Savio.

"It's a pleasure to see you," said Matthew, shaking Savio's hand. "And how strange! I hadn't thought I'd make it here."

"And here I am at the very same hour on the very same day!" said Savio. "Extraordinary!"

Matthew introduced Fernando, and explained that they were heading off—that he would soon be catching a plane for England.

"For England!" said Savio. "Dear me, but you do get around! But before you go there's something here I must show you. It's too droll." Amused but captivated by Savio's enthusiasm, Matthew and Fernando followed Savio around one of the central structures and towards a building closer to the perimeter. "This is just so strange," said Savio. "There's a place here, a kind of temple, where they used to perform human sacrifices. They would take the leaders of their enemies into this underground chamber and castrate them—imagine that! And we know that, because here, at the entrance, we actually see artistic representations of the poor buggers they castrated!" He waved toward a series of stone reliefs, and Matthew saw that this was true. "What a horrible way to go, eh?" said Savio. "Though maybe they drugged them first. Let's say they did!"

"I doubt they did," said Fernando.

"No?" said Savio. "No wine on a sponge for the *castrati*? Well, that's savage, then. Come inside with me, Matthew." He gestured toward a door leading into the building. "We can't go far—it's all walled off—but there's something deliciously *macabre* about going into a passage where such ghastly things took place."

Savio was speaking differently, Matthew registered, from how he had spoken on the plane: there was a touch of the manic about him. But there was no doubting his delight at seeing Matthew, or his ebullient good will. Matthew didn't have any real interest in seeing the site of ritual castrations, but . . . "Sure," Matthew said. "You coming, Fernando?"

"No, thank you," said Fernando. "I have some claustrophobia. You go ahead. I'll finish my water and wait out here in the sun."

"After you, Matthew," said Savio gaily, gesturing with a flourish—and Matthew stooped a little, then stepped through the door and made his way along the passage.

CHAPTER TWENTY-FOUR

M atthew had expected that the passage would be short, and that he would soon come to the walled-off area, but he found himself walking farther and farther, and he was uncomfortable because he was bent over at the waist. Surprisingly, too, for a publicly-accessible site, there was very little lighting: there were lamps built into the side of the walls, but they were some distance apart and their bulbs were dull. "How long before we come to the end?" he asked Savio, who was right behind him.

"Isn't it *delicious*?" said Savio. "I think it's *wonderful* that the museum authorities allow us to go so far along. I just wish we could see the ritual chamber itself—but it's probably still being excavated!"

"Mmm," said Matthew, not fully persuaded. "The whole set-up must be a real nightmare when the site is crowded, though. There's not really enough room for two modern-sized people to pass each other. How do they control traffic in and out?"

"I hadn't thought of that," said Savio brightly, "but I'm sure it's regulated somehow. Probably the tour guides have a schedule."

They walked on, Matthew increasingly feeling the strain of bending over in his lower back. The passage had begun to slope downward, too, and he realized that the return journey would be more difficult. "How much farther now, Savio?" he asked.

"Just a little," said Savio. "The barrier is just a minute away—three or four more lamps and we're there. So *exciting!*"

There was something in the way that Savio pronounced *exciting* that made Matthew stop suddenly. It just didn't sound right—a creak in a solid oak floor, a flat note in an aria. "I'm going to use my phone as a flashlight," he said, buying a moment to think.

"Oh, what a good idea," said Savio, "but as I recall there's a lamp just around the next bend—"

But at that moment Matthew wheeled around and shone his cell's light on Savio's face. Savio recoiled, and in recoiling jerked his head back—and that abrupt movement caused just the slightest slippage in what Matthew now saw was a wig. And something about the way Savio's face settled when he brought it back level reminded Matthew of another face—a face he'd spent a fair bit of time studying, looking for clues. It was the face of the man sitting beside Hannah Hutchinson at the wedding in Huajuapan.

"So," said Savio, almost hissing, "I think my little secret may be out—" and with that he swung his left hand at Matthew's wrist, seeking to knock the cell phone away, and followed up swiftly by barreling into the detective and punching at his testicles: for a short, slight man he was stunningly strong. But Matthew was not weak, and he'd had an instant to brace himself. He jerked his phone away from Savio's swing, and grabbed the hand that reached for his groin, bending it back, back, back—and he would have been fine, would have had the upper hand quickly, but someone jumped him from behind and he went down. Whoever had jumped him was bigger and heavier than Savio, and he sat astride Matthew and put his hands around his neck, feeling for the carotid artery. Before he could find it, however, Matthew summoned the strength first to rear up, then to roll over, breaking the hold on his neck, though with a quick shift of weight his attacker remained on top of him. "Hold him for just a second longer—" Savio's voice—but then Savio gave a shout of dismay, and Matthew was aware that a *fourth* person had entered the fray and was now wrestling with Savio.

"Matthew! Are you there?"—Fernando's voice in the dark!

"Fernando! Yes!" said Matthew, and he aimed a volley of punches up at the person sitting astride him, who, though he successfully protected his face and neck, decided to push away from Matthew and get out of the range of his fists.

"Are you free?" asked Fernando. Matthew guessed from the strain in his voice that he'd got the better of Savio, but was having to restrain him.

"Yes!" said Matthew. "Can you head for the exit? I think I can."

A weird popping noise came out of the darkness, then— "Go! said Fernando. "Go, go! Savio is on the ground—don't trip over him!"

There was a scrambling noise, and Matthew guessed that Fernando had let go of Savio and was heading back towards the outside. He got to his own feet, grabbed his phone from the ground, nearly tripped over a recumbent body, then moved as swiftly as he could along the passage, conscious that Fernando was only a metre ahead. "I'm right behind you, Fernando," he said, gasping for breath, "and I don't think they're following us."

"Savio will not follow us," said Fernando, a grim note in his own voice. "I think his neck is broken." And as Matthew was absorbing the significance of this, the two of them stumbled out into the light.

"Thank you!" said Matthew. "I couldn't have handled both of them—"

"We must leave here *now*," Fernando cut in. "I don't know who these people are, but we are not safe."

The two men did not run, but their pace was brisk. In four minutes they had reached the stone steps leading to the ramparts.

"How did you know to come in?" asked Matthew beginning his ascent.

"I was suspicious," said Fernando. "When I was here as a student the passage was just a few metres long and there was nothing to see. And I didn't like your friend Savio."

"He's no friend of mine," said Matthew, clenching his jaw.

They climbed the steps quickly, urgency lending them both energy and breath. Across the grassy verge—past trees with white flowers that Matthew had not really registered before, and only noticed now because he was intensely awake—then down the steps leading to the ticket booth—and suddenly the sound of police sirens. "Fuck," said Fernando.

They kept going: the police had probably pulled up in the parking lot and it would take them a minute or two to get up to where Matthew and Fernando were. There was a large crowd in the assembly area: evidently a good many tourists were not put off by the gathering heat. As the two approached the fringes of the crowd a number of policemen erupted up the steps. "We have a problem," said Fernando.

At that moment, a figure Matthew recognized detached herself from the crowd: Reverend Clara! She was, Matthew saw, just in front of a group of other ministers, all of them sun-hatted, but also wearing button-up shirts and white clerical collars, which must have been formidably uncomfortable in the July sun.

"Matthew!" cried Clara. "What a lovely surprise to see you here!" She beckoned to them both.

CHAPTER TWENTY-FIVE

"Clara," said Matthew, "We're—"

"We'll just put these on you and Fernando," said Clara, pulling two clerical collars from her handbag. "Jane, can you look after Fernando, while I attend to Matthew?" Another woman was instantly at Fernando's side, fitting a collar round his neck. It was Jane—Jane from the coffee shop in Toronto. Jane the dominatrix. "And they'll need nice, touristy hats," said Clara. Two straw hats were produced by someone behind her, and she and Jane arranged them jauntily on Matthew and Fernando's heads while the group of clergy, perhaps twenty strong, surged around them, chatting and laughing and taking pictures of each other, while the Mexican police passed by, rushing toward the central plaza. One young officer stopped and looked suspiciously at the ministers, whereupon Clara forged through the crowd, stood in front of him, and pinned a little bronze cross on his uniform.

"We are all visiting from Canada," she said, beaming at him, "and we are so impressed with the dedication of Mexican peace officers. You are an inspiration to us all! Go with God, my child." The policeman looked thoroughly bewildered, but his suspicions seemed to dissipate, and he ran off behind his colleagues. "Now," said Clara, moving toward Fernando and Matthew, her fellow clergy—if that's what they were—parting for her. "The two of you must be off. Fernando, take Matthew to the airport, then go straight home and stay there for the next couple of days: the danger to you will blow over. And Matthew, you have a plane to catch."

Matthew stared at Clara. *Who is this woman?* he wondered. *What is this woman?* He shook his head. "Can we trust that Hannah is in England?" he asked.

"Yes," said Clara. "But be very careful." She raised her hand and placed her fingers lightly on Fernando's forehead. "You don't need to remember everything, Fernando," she said. "Let some things slip away." Then, to both of them, "Go."

The journey from Monte Alban to the airport took a little over half an hour. Matthew and Fernando were mostly silent during the journey, each separately reflecting on the events of the last hour.

"You knew that woman?" said Fernando, at one point.

"Yes," said Matthew. "We met in Canada a few days ago."

"But how does she know my name?" asked Fernando. "And what is she doing in Oaxaca?"

"I don't know," said Matthew. "I'm as surprised as you are."

When the airport terminal came in sight, Matthew pulled out his wallet. He counted fifteen one thousand-peso notes and tucked them into Fernando's shirt pocket.

"It's too much," said Fernando, who had seen the count out of the corner of his eye.

"No, it isn't," said Matthew. He reached into the back seat for his suitcase. "Can you take the car back to the hotel for me?"

"Of course," said Fernando, pulling up in the passenger drop-off area.

"It's been a pleasure meeting you," said Matthew, shaking Fernando's hand. "I'm sorry that I got you into something so messy and dangerous. I had no idea."

"It was an interesting two days," said Fernando.

"Savio should not be on your conscience," said Matthew.

Fernando looked puzzled. "Savio?" he said.

"The man in the tunnel—" Matthew began, but he stopped. Clearly Savio was someone Fernando did not need to remember. "Well, we met some fine people, didn't we?" he said. "I really enjoyed meeting your friends."

"They are good people," said Fernando, smiling.

Matthew climbed out of the car with his suitcase, closed the door, and waved Fernando off. He then went into the terminal, checking his phone as he did to see just what his options might be. To his astonishment, he found there was a direct flight to

Manchester in three hours, and further exploration revealed that he would be able to catch a train from Manchester to Salisbury through London. The prospect of spending the next sixteen hours, including wait times, in transit did not warm his heart, but it was good to know it was all possible. He bought his ticket, passed through security, and stepped into the arrivals and departures lounge, hoping he might find a comfortable place to sit, read, and, perhaps, nap. A comfortable place in the lounge was too much to ask for, but he set himself up in a chair with a cup of surprisingly good airport coffee and launched back into Dr. Pagel's book. He'd been reading for twenty minutes, his blood pressure just about back to normal, when two police officers entered the lounge and circulated among the passengers waiting for their flights. Eventually they made their way to him.

"*Buenas tardes, Señor,*" said the shorter of the two men.

"Good afternoon," said Matthew. "I'm afraid I speak very little Spanish."

The shorter man looked stymied by this, but the other officer spoke up immediately. "May we ask what you were doing in Oaxaca?"

Though Matthew had removed his straw hat, he was still wearing his clerical collar, and he saw that he would need to stick with that persona, whatever the risks might be. "I was here with a group of Canadian ministers," he said. "We were visiting churches and meeting with priests in Oaxaca City."

"And why are you not travelling with that group now?" asked the officer.

"I have been called back early," said Matthew. "A family emergency."

"I am sorry to hear that, Señor. Your passport and ticket, please."

Matthew felt a moment of contained panic. His passport would not present a problem, but his ticket was for England, not Canada. He quickly began the process of inventing an elderly mother and father living in the United Kingdom. A heart attack? A broken hip? An automobile accident? What crisis would require him to abandon a clerical junket?

But at that moment there was a commotion at the far end of the lounge. A woman in traditional indigenous clothing had apparently failed to receive what she'd paid for from a vending machine, and she kicked the offending machine several times, swearing loudly. A cashier rushed to restrain her, but the woman pushed her away. *"Policia! Policia! He sido robado!"* she shouted. It seemed likely that she was either on drugs or experiencing some sort of mental disturbance.

The two police officers looked at each other, then turned away from Matthew and hastened toward the raving woman and the cashier. When she saw them coming, she launched into a dramatic dance, stamping her feet and swiveling her hips, to music only she could hear. She fought back hard when they tried to handcuff her, but within a couple of minutes they were hustling her out of the lounge and, perhaps, to some sort of detention or medical facility.

Matthew watched them go with a mixture of relief and concern. At the last moment he recognized the agitated woman who had spared him, at the very least, a prolonged interrogation. It was Mariela, the pretty young woman with whom the tour guides at Monte Alban checked in.

CHAPTER TWENTY-SIX

About an hour before boarding, two hundred English and Irish holiday-makers poured into the airport lounge: they had apparently flown in from the coast, where they'd spent a well-lubricated week at a new resort. Fortunately, they were happy drunks, and many of them seemed to have formed strong intercultural friendships. "This is my great chum Paddy," a large Englishman announced to no one in particular. "He's Irish, but I love the son-of-a-bitch!" And Paddy, if that were indeed his name—which struck Matthew as *very* unlikely—hugged the Englishman and announced that Stanley and his mates were welcome in Ireland any time, and that their children should all get married and that then there would be world peace. So it was a merry band that boarded the Virgin Airlines flight for Manchester, and the merriment lasted for a good three hours until, mid-Atlantic, most of the group fell fast asleep.

Matthew's seat-mates for the flight were a comparatively contained couple from Bath, who seemed a little embarrassed by their compatriots' behaviour. "We had fun," said Gerald, who had something to do with food wholesaling, "but they shouldn't have allowed drinking on the airport bus. Not in the morning." And Ethel, his wife, agreed: "Some people can't hold their drink," she said. "I'm sure you don't have that problem in Canada."

"I'm afraid we do," said Matthew wryly. "Isn't summer an odd time of year to visit a beach resort?" he added. "Surely summer is a good time to be in England."

"It was cheap," said Gerald, "and Ethel and I like a bargain—don't we, Ethel?"

"We like a good bargain," Ethel confirmed. "And we get a lot of American visitors in the summer, so it's good to get away for a week."

"Not that we have anything against Americans," said Gerald. "But they're very loud."

At that moment Stanley, or one of his mates, began to snore with great rumbling resonance three rows back. Matthew smiled, covered himself with a complimentary blanket, and did his best to sleep.

They landed in Manchester at 7:30 in the morning, Matthew found the railway station easily, and had only minutes to wait for a train to Manchester Piccadilly. Eighteen minutes to drink a tea and read a newspaper, then he was off on the next leg to London Euston. A quick trip on the Tube to London Waterloo, and ten minutes on the platform before catching the train to Salisbury— a ninety-minute journey. During his time on the London Waterloo platform, Matthew surveyed his bed-and-breakfast options online, eventually opting for The White Dove, a place just a few minutes' walk from the cathedral.

The day was warm and sunny, and had he not been jet-lagged, Matthew would have enjoyed his views of the English cityscapes and countryside. On the last leg of his journey, he was joined, at the last moment, by a gentleman in his late seventies or early eighties. He was white-haired, somewhat wizened, a little stooped—but with piercing, bright blue eyes. Matthew sized him up as he sat down, swiftly deciding that whoever he might be, he did not represent a physical threat. He nodded to Matthew, then retreated inside himself until the fellow selling refreshments came around. He and Matthew both ordered tea and a cheese sandwich.

"You're not English," said the older gentleman. It was an observation, not a challenge.

"No, I'm from Canada," said Matthew.

"But your ancestors were English," said the gentleman.

"Yes, mostly," said Matthew, "but that's going back a couple of generations. Are you English yourself?"

"Oh, yes," said his seat-companion. "This has been my home since the dawn of time." He laughed. "I'm old," he added.

"Well, you carry the years lightly," said Matthew.

"That is most gracious of you. And you are planning to visit the cathedral?"

"Yes," said Matthew. "It's not the reason for my trip, but I certainly hope to see it. It's something I've wanted to visit for a long, long time."

"It's worth the trip," said the gentleman with the piercing bright blue eyes. "And you'll see Stonehenge, too. And Old Sarum."

"I hope so," said Matthew. "Tell me, do you know of any archeological excavations in the area? Are any sites open to the public?"

The old gentleman looked sideways at him. "To the northeast," he said. "Along what they call Stonehenge Avenue."

"Can one visit?" asked Matthew.

"One can, but it's probably not necessary," said the gentleman. "There's only so much one can absorb in a couple of days."

"Ah," said Matthew, unsure of how to take this.

"I have something to give you."

Matthew's heart sunk. Some years previous he'd been on a Greyhound bus just outside Calgary, Alberta, and a lovely young woman had struck up a conversation with him. They had been getting along famously when suddenly she had used those very words, *I have something to give you*, and handed him a fundamentalist tract with the title, *You're Going to Hell . . . Unless*. "Uh, okay," he said, warily.

The old gentleman reached into the left pocket of his trousers and withdrew a tiny box. It was the size of box that might hold an engagement ring or a set of diamond earrings, but it appeared to be hand-carved and hand-polished. He handed it to Matthew.

Matthew looked at it, then at his seat-mate. "It's a beautiful box," he said. "Is there anything inside it?"

"The best way to find out is to open it," said the old fellow gently.

Matthew opened the box. Inside was a small vial—cylindrical and made of glass—containing a clear liquid. "I'm not sure I'm any the wiser," said Matthew.

"It's a few drops of water from a spring on Ynys Enlli," said the old gentleman. "A holy place off the coast of Wales."

"Ah," said Matthew. "Thank you."

"You're a modern man, my friend," said his companion, "but I think you know that there is more to the world than what you can see and touch and taste. This may be useful to you, but if it isn't, I'm just a harmless old British eccentric you met on the train on your way to Salisbury—and you have a nice little wooden box as a memento of your trip."

"Thank you, again," said Matthew, and he met the old gentleman's gaze, smiled, then put the box securely in the pocket of his jacket. At that moment, their tea and sandwiches arrived, and they had no further conversation while they ate and drank. As they neared Salisbury, the old fellow got up, patted Matthew's shoulder, and headed off down the aisle. He did not return.

Chapter Twenty-Seven

The White Dove bed-and-breakfast was located on a quiet street in residential Salisbury, and the front door was opened by a striking Indian woman wearing a sari. "Welcome," she said, "my name is Alia." She shook hands firmly, then led him to his room, which was decorated in blues and golds, with a queen-size bed, an armoire, an expensive-looking radio, and an ensuite bathroom.

"This is wonderful," said Matthew. "Are there many other guests?"

"I think there will just be three of you tonight," said Alia. "There's a charming young couple from Leeds on the other side of the hall. You'll probably meet them at breakfast."

"I look forward to that," said Matthew, politely. "My challenge is going to be staying awake until this evening."

"I've travelled a lot," said Alia, "and I've never believed in just powering through jet lag. You should have an afternoon sleep, if you need one."

"I may well," said Matthew. "I'm running on fumes at the moment."

"We don't have televisions in the rooms," said Alia, "but, as you see, you do have a good radio, and there is a small library downstairs. Please feel free to help yourself to a volume." And she left, with a swish of her sari, leaving the scent of vanilla and lemons in her wake.

Following a hot shower and a shave, Matthew sat on a chair by his bedside and contemplated his options. It was still too early in Ontario to call either Sharon or Andrew, but he sent Sharon a brief email, telling her where he was, and promising to check in later that day. He deliberated for a moment over how to end his message. *Warm thoughts? Take care?* Not appropriate for an employer, he decided, and closed with a simple *Best*—bloodless, but safe. And now . . . next steps. He didn't know anyone in Salisbury, but he did have a private investigator colleague in London—someone he'd collaborated with, via phone and email, years and years before. He called his office, identified himself to the investigator's receptionist, and she patched him through. "Rory," Matthew said, "I could use your help. Do you have any contacts in Salisbury?" He outlined his problem.

Rory listened to Matthew's inquiries, then told him he knew a man who might be able to help. "Let me call you back in ten," he said. Matthew hung up, then laid down on the bed to close his eyes for a few minutes. He was jolted awake, almost immediately, with the news that Rory had called his contact, and that Matthew could reach him at such-and-such a number. Matthew thanked him, then made another call.

John Deacon wasn't immediately available, so Matthew left a message on his answering service, noting with interest that John identified himself as a Missing Persons Consultant rather than a private investigator or private detective. While he waited to hear back, he wrote an email to Andrew, bringing him up to date. He left out the death of Savio, saying simply that he and his guide had been mugged, but had escaped unscathed. To his surprise, an email from Sharon dropped into his box as he was writing. *Glad you've arrived safely,* it said. *You must be so tired. Take care of yourself. Big hug from Canada. Sharon.* The warmth of the message briefly assuaged his fatigue. His mind's eye conjured up a pleasant picture of Sharon at his side, looking intently at the photograph of Hannah on his computer screen.

Matthew's phone interrupted his reverie, and he fumbled a little while answering it—revealing to himself that jet lag was affecting his coordination. The caller was John Deacon, who was about an hour away at that moment, but due back in town in the late afternoon. Matthew offered to buy him dinner anywhere in Salisbury, and John suggested the Ox Row Inn.

And that left the bulk of the afternoon. There was a huge temptation to sleep, but Matthew had told the old gentleman on the train the truth when he said he'd wanted to visit Salisbury

Cathedral for years. He stretched, yawned, then went downstairs, where Alia, possibly relieved to see him looking less grizzled and unkempt, was happy to give him directions to the cathedral.

Salisbury Cathedral has the highest spire of any church in Britain, and is surrounded by fields and trees. Matthew felt a rising excitement as he approached the building: impressive from a distance, it was, he found, almost overwhelming up close. It was when he stepped inside, however, that he found himself in tears. Canada is a beautiful country: its mountains and lakes are miracles of nature, its prairies endless, its major cities impressively modern. What it lacks is breathtaking ecclesiastical architecture—buildings designed and engineered to suggest the glory of God. The nave of Salisbury Cathedral with its impossibly high ceiling, its majestic arches, its stunning stained-glass windows, left Matthew speechless.

While he was wandering slack-jawed around the cathedral, he was accosted by a woman who he guessed to be Romany, a gypsy, in her late-thirties. "Would you have a pound or two for an old woman to get herself a cup of tea?" she asked, tugging at the ends of her long shawl.

Matthew smiled. "You're not what I would call an old woman, ma'am," he said, digging in his pocket, "but I'm happy to give you a couple of pounds."

"Might you have another pound or three so I can buy my boy there a glass of milk and a sandwich?" the woman said, gesturing toward a little boy standing near the baptismal font.

Matthew dug in his pocket and found three more loose pounds, which he handed to the woman. She held them in her hand with the first two, looking Matthew in the eyes all the while.

"And do you have another five pounds to spare for those who are lost and hungry and afraid in this island kingdom?" she said.

Matthew hesitated, then looked around him. The sun was shining brilliantly through the cathedral's glass windows. He had never been in such an awe-inspiring man-made space before. He pulled out his wallet, found a ten-pound note, and handed it to her.

"God bless you, sir," she said.

"God bless you, ma'am," he replied, recognizing that he'd just been the subject of a particularly artful con.

"Put the water in the font, then dip your hands in," said the woman in a low voice, then she gathered her shawl around her, held her hand out for the boy, and left the cathedral.

CHAPTER TWENTY-EIGHT

Put the water in the font, then dip your hands in, Matthew repeated to himself. *Put the water in the font? What on earth could she mean?* And then he realized that her reference might be to the vial of water he'd been given by the old gentleman on the train. His hand strayed into his pocket and he found the little wooden box and caressed it. But another thought came into his mind: it had been only a year since Russian SVR agents had poisoned two Russian dissidents right here in Salisbury. The last thing Matthew wanted to do was to pour some unknown liquid into a font where children would be baptized. The idea was crazy.

And yet. He felt in his gut that the old gentleman on the train had not been in any way dangerous. He believed, as a corollary, that the water was, as he'd been told, just water—albeit, perhaps, from a special spring. And how could the woman know what the old man had given him, unless she was in some way connected to him? And what would be the harm of adding a little water to water if it was simply water? (Though what on earth would be the point?) And what had been the significance of her speaking of "the lost and hungry and afraid"—was that, perhaps, a reference to Hannah? And was he so jet-lagged, and so overwhelmed by the strange events of the last few days, and by the weirdness of his dreams, that he was incapable of thinking clearly? *Step back, step back,* he told himself. *You're disoriented. You're discombobulated.* His mind played crazily with both words, making a tuneless, nonsense song out of them.

You're disoriented
You're discombobulated
You're simply overrated
You're the top!

Matthew did not empty his vial of water in the font—but he met the Romany woman halfway. He went to the font, leaned forward and dipped the fingertips of his right hand into the water, then walked over to the row of seats nearby and sat down. He took out the box, placed it in his lap, opened it, removed the vial, then uncorked it and spilled some of its water into his left palm, into which he rubbed his fingertips still damp from the font. He then rubbed his hands together, so that traces of the two waters were effectively spread all over his hands. *This is silly*, he thought. *Just plain daft. Assuming it's not poison, I'm practicing a kind of spiritual homeopathy.* He stared at his hands: they looked completely normal. They felt completely normal. He sniffed them. They smelled normal. He tucked the vial back in the box, closed the box, slipped it back in his pocket, and walked out into the sunshine.

The sun was still shining, but he'd been inside longer than he realized. Matthew checked his phone, saw that he still had an hour before his meeting with John, and took the opportunity to walk around the cathedral close, the walk giving him the opportunity to view the building from every angle. He spent some time studying the bronze sculpture of the walking Madonna, her two-metre frame slightly larger than life, her figure slender and her face profoundly sad. Matthew felt moved to reach out and take her hand, but though he resisted the temptation to hold on to it, he did allow his fingers to touch hers—and in doing so he felt a small jolt, a gentle burst of something like electricity. *You're cracking up, boyo*, he thought.

But if he was cracking up, he was, at minimum, attentive to his professional responsibilities. He reread the email from Sharon, and read a brief message of thanks from Andrew, as he sat on the grass looking up at the Madonna, and at 5:40 he checked Google to give him directions to the Ox Row Inn. And just a little later, he reluctantly turned his back on the cathedral, and set off to meet John Deacon.

★ ★ ★

Deacon was a large, bluff, friendly man in his mid-fifties. He arrived a few minutes after Matthew had staked out a table near the door, shook his hand firmly, ordered a beer and fish and chips, then paid close attention to Matthew's story—holding back his questions until Matthew had finished. "So," he said, "you want to know if Hannah Hutchinson is in Salisbury, or nearby, and, if so, precisely where she is."

"Is that something you can help me with?" asked Matthew.

"I think so," said John. "Since the Russian poisonings this town has been plastered with CCTV cameras. If Ms. Hutchinson has entered Salisbury even once, the cameras will have recorded her."

"Do you have access to these cameras?" asked Matthew.

"Not officially. But I worked for the police for thirty years, and some of my old colleagues will help me out if they know what I'm doing is on the side of the angels. They're a good bunch, the security lads."

"That's excellent news," said Matthew. "You understand that I have to raise the issue of costs with you? My client is not a wealthy man, and I need to spend his resources carefully."

The fish and chips arrived while John mulled this over. "Tell you what," he said, after the waiter had departed, "I'll cheerfully help you out for a couple of dinners, cab fare when I've had a drink too many, and the promise of a couch in Toronto if I ever visit there. I don't like to think of more trouble coming to Salisbury."

"That's very generous," said Matthew. "And I have a guest bedroom." The two men shook on it. Matthew emailed John his photos of Hannah and the link to the video.

"You realize I'll be sharing these with my own contacts?" John said.

"Mr. Greenfield would be all right with that," said Matthew.

"She's a sweet-looking lass," said John, scrolling through the photos. "I can see why her man would be desperate to get her back." Ten minutes later they went their separate ways, John to meet with a former colleague, and Matthew to his bed and breakfast.

At the back of the Inn's dining room, an East Asian teenager and a broad-shouldered young man called for their bill, and slipped out of the pub.

CHAPTER TWENTY-NINE

Matthew returned to his bed-and-breakfast, meeting Alia in the front hall as he came in. "Have you had a pleasant afternoon?" she asked him.

"Yes," he replied. "I visited the cathedral. It's extraordinary."

"Isn't it?" said Alia. "And will you see Stonehenge tomorrow?"

"I hope so," said Matthew, "but it's possible some business may intervene." He removed his shoes—something he hadn't thought of doing when he first arrived. Alia looked pleased.

"Breakfast is between eight and nine," she said. "The Malcoviches—that's the young couple from Leeds—said they'd be down right at 8:00."

"Fair enough," said Matthew. "I prefer an early start myself. Good night, Mrs.—" He paused.

"Alia," she said. "Just call me Alia, Matthew. I hope you sleep well."

Matthew went up to his room and wallowed in the bath. He relaxed for a few minutes, but discovered that he was in grave danger of falling asleep and dropping his book in the water, so he dried off, put on a fresh pair of underwear, and slipped into bed. "I'll read for ten minutes," he said aloud, but he was asleep in two.

He swam back into a kind of consciousness in another lucid dream. He was on a lightly-wooded slope, and there was a large crowd of people in front of him but on the other side of a stream. They were listening to someone, he could not see who, but the voice was male, passionate, compelling. He desperately wanted to hear more clearly. He walked toward the stream, trying to assess how deep it was, and whether he could cross safely.

As he came to the bank, he saw two men at the back of the crowd on the opposite side turn away from the speaker and look at him. It was—inevitably—the broad-shouldered young man and the East Asian teenager. They both had staves. They stood, shoulder-to-shoulder, facing him across the water. "Come on across, Matthew," said the broad-shouldered man, mockingly.

Matthew stepped into the stream, which was surprisingly deep, and began to move forward—but immediately felt something lock onto his submerged thighs. He looked down and there, just below the surface, was the pallid face of Savio Malise leering up at him. An instant later he was pulled down, down into a stream that had suddenly become oceanic in its depth, and he found himself locked in a death struggle with an animated corpse—

He woke up gasping for air.

CHAPTER THIRTY

Matthew slept fitfully, when he slept at all. Savio's colourless face kept reappearing—dead but leering, lifeless but threatening. At 4:00 a.m. Matthew gave up trying to sleep and got up to read. He read a good half of Pagels' book in the next couple of hours, falling into a kind of fretful slumber in his chair. His phone rang at 7:30.

"Matthew? It's John. Did I wake you?"

"No," said Matthew automatically, the cragginess of his voice betraying the truth. He cleared his throat. "Sorry. Yes. Bad night. Jet lag."

"I understand," said John sympathetically. "Listen, I have news. Your lass was spotted two days ago going through the backdoor of a club called Busy Bodies. She came out again six hours, twenty-two minutes later."

"Okay," said Matthew. "What sort of a club is Busy Bodies? I'm guessing it's not a children's birthday party place."

"No," said John. "It's an adult entertainment club. And that's a euphemism."

"Strippers?"

"Well, it's a full-service operation," said John. "Stripping is the low end—table dances. But also happy-ending massage. Oral. Full one-on-one. More exotic delights."

"Great," said Matthew, deadpan.

"So my guess is that she's being coerced somehow," said John. "Most of the girls there are east European, with a few brought in from Syria and Afghanistan. It's run by a couple of Pakistani gentlemen. I use the word loosely."

"Why the hell is it allowed to operate?" asked Matthew.

"The girls aren't underage," said John flatly. "That's the dif-ference from the Rochdale thing. The police have tried to infiltrate it, but these fellas are cagey. They can sniff an under-cover a mile away."

"I have to speak to her," Matthew said. "If I can see her one-on-one, I can ask if she needs help getting out. I'll tell her Andrew sent me."

"It's not going to be easy, Matthew," said John. "They get the girls hooked on speed or whatever, and they're terrified to have their supply stopped."

"I have to try," said Matthew.

"Okay," said John. "The place opens at 1:00. They'll know who I am, so there's no point in me going. Sit at a table. Order a beer. See if you can spot her among the other girls."

"Maybe it would be good if you were there, too," said Matthew. "You might take their attention off me."

"Maybe," said John. "Maybe. Okay. I'll go at 1:10. You come at 1:20. We'll sit at opposite sides of the room." Matthew wrote down the address and ended the call.

The Malcoviches turned out to be from Leeds only in the sense that that's where they lived for the moment. They were, in fact, fellow Canadians, and, like Matthew, from Toronto.

"We're both doing grad work at the University of Leeds," said Julie Malcovich. "I'm doing an MA in Post-Colonial Studies." She was a large woman with her hair dyed purple on one half of her head.

Matthew nodded. "What are you studying, Craig?" he asked.

"Chemistry," said Craig. Tall and thin, he had a high, rather reedy voice. "I'm interested in the properties of water."

"From an environmental perspective?" asked Matthew.

"Not so much," said Craig. "At least—not directly. I'm interested in its molecular structure. I'm testing to see whether it changes when it's exposed to different kinds of music."

"I remember reading that a Japanese researcher suggested that a few years back," Matthew said.

"Oh, yes, there's a wonderful video on YouTube!" said Julie. "You must watch it. I showed it to Craig. That's what got him started."

"But I honestly thought the theory had been, er, debunked," said Matthew.

Craig shifted uneasily in his seat. "It's difficult to be definitive about it," he said. "I mean, the molecular structure of water is H2o, it's pretty straightforward. But some interesting things sometimes happen when it freezes. The crystals can look very different depending on what they're exposed to. But Dr. Emoto—he was the Japanese researcher—Dr. Emoto may have been highly . . . *selective* in the photos he published."

"Where did you do your undergraduate work?" asked Matthew, sensing some tension between Craig and his wife.

"York," said Julie. "Great place."

"This is York in Toronto?"

"Oh, yes," said Julie, "we've never even visited York in the UK."

"Was it a good experience?" Matthew asked.

"I really enjoyed it," said Julie. "I didn't go to class much, but I was very involved with BDS and anti-Zionism work. I even got some academic credit for it."

"That doesn't happen in the Sciences," said Craig.

"This is very good jam, Alia," Matthew said. "Is it home-made?" Alia had just entered the room with a fresh pot of tea.

"It is," said Alia, smiling, "But not by me. My sister makes it."

"We also did a lot of work with the gender-neutral campaign," said Julie. "We're both gender fluid."

"Well, I'm not really—" Craig began.

"Craig's an ally," said Julie. "He went to all the dances and demos with me." Craig acknowledged this with a little bob of the head.

"The best of luck to both of you," said Matthew, rising. "Could I possibly take my tea to go, Alia?"

CHAPTER THIRTY-ONE

M atthew was torn between visiting Salisbury cathedral again, or seeing Stonehenge. There no longer seemed a need to visit the archeological digs to the north, but he was very curious to see the ancient stone circle. With a view to spending as much time there as possible he took a taxi, and was driven by a pleasant Pakistani gentleman who, he was confident, had no involvement whatsoever with Busy Bodies or any business like it. Mr. Malik gave Matthew a well-informed history of the stones, telling him that construction probably began around 3100 B.C., but likely spanned fifteen hundred years; that the large standing stones might have come from a quarry twenty-five miles away, and the blue-stones in the inner circle from the Presili Hills in what is now Wales, one hundred and fifty miles away; that the site's origins predated the druids who are sometimes wrongly credited with its creation; that it was, among other things, a burial site; and that the whole complex was much larger than what we now see. "It is a place from the Bronze Age, sir, and very fascinating," he concluded. "It is remarkable that it survived, and we are very proud of it." Matthew thanked him for the background, and tipped him generously.

Though Mr. Malik dropped him off at the visitor centre, Matthew was not moved to explore it. After buying his ticket he boarded the shuttle for the site, disembarking halfway, with a number of other people, to walk the remaining distance. Doing so meant that the stones came gradually into view as he ascended a slope. A young Japanese couple were just ahead of him, and he listened with pleasure to the musical quality of their *oohs* and *ahhs* as they drew nearer. Two children of nine or ten ran ahead of their parents, stopped, and looked back: "It's not as big as I thought it would be," one of them called. "No, it's bigger!" said the other. Then they turned and raced ahead again. There was, Matthew saw, a crowd of people assembled at the first point at which one could get close to the site, many folk taking photos or videos with their cell phones or cameras. He joined them, but kept his cell in his pocket.

"I don't understand why they said it could be a calendar," said a young woman standing near him to a female friend.

"I think it's got something to do with the summer solstice," said her friend. "On June twenty-first the sun shines right into the middle of the ring—or something like that."

"And they went to all this trouble just for *that*?" asked the first young woman.

"No, it's a burial site, too," said the friend.

"So who built it?" asked the first woman, who had clearly not read any of the brochures or placards on offer.

"Now there's a question," murmured a voice in Matthew's ear. Matthew glanced to his side, and there was the old gentleman—the one with the piercing, bright blue eyes, from the train.

"I want to say it's a startling coincidence to see you again," said Matthew, "but I suspect it isn't."

"Well, perhaps not," said the old gentleman, "but, you know, extremely improbable events happen all the time. Let's call it *synchronicity* in this case, shall we?"

"Synchronicity," Matthew said. "Okay. What brings you here?"

"I come here often," said the old gentleman. He stared at the stones. "We live in a wondrous world, Matthew," he continued. "There are accidents and deliberate acts. There are powers for good, and powers for evil. Your own path has become intertwined with an evil whose name I am loath even to speak. But, Matthew," he looked directly at him: "you are not alone. You have help. And that help will come from different places and draw on very different sources of strength."

"Fair enough," said Matthew, "but who are you? I don't want to seem ungrateful for anything you're offering me, but who in God's name are you?"

"Sir, you dropped your ticket," said a voice at Matthew's elbow. He turned, and there was one of the young lads who had run on ahead of his parents earlier. He was holding up a ticket to the site. "It fell out of your pocket," he said.

"Thank you very much," said Matthew, smiling at the boy. The young boy nodded and ran back to his family. Matthew turned back to the old man.

But he was gone.

★ ★ ★

At 1:20 that afternoon, Matthew entered the Busy Bodies club. He was sized up by a large and muscular man with a shaved head, who quickly judged that Matthew didn't pose a threat and was likely to spend money. A short entrance hallway quickly opened up into a large room, dimly-lit but with spotlights on a small stage jutting out from one of the walls. It was early in the day for a club of this kind, but there were already about fifteen customers, all male, most seated alone at small tables or tucked away in recessed booths. A topless young woman was gyrating to Tina Turner's "What's Love Got to Do with It" on the stage, and two others were dancing on little boxes at different tables, both of them approaching complete nudity. The music was fairly loud; not so loud as to frustrate conversation at a table, but loud enough that conversations would not be overheard between tables.

It was not Matthew's first visit to a strip club, but his visits were rare enough that he was alive to the sad nature of the spectacle. Here were young women—sleek, slender, manicured, pedicured, perfumed, gorgeous. Here also were mostly, though not exclusively, middle-aged men, often tired-looking, rumpled, hang-doggish. The women were often young enough to be the daughters of the customers. The conventional wisdom, of course, was that all the power resided with the men: that money gave them access to the young women's sexuality, to their most private places, but Matthew knew that it was more complicated than that—that men left such places more lonely, more sexually frustrated, more self-loathing and poorer than they went in. But that, of course, was true only if a club just offered stripping; if other "services" were available, then the power equation changed. Always, of course, the chief beneficiaries of the system were the men who managed such places, whether they were strip clubs or brothels. And things were much, much worse if the women were essentially prisoners, kept in servitude by their addiction to heroin or crack cocaine. And then, of course, there was the other side of the equation—bright, empowered young women who put themselves through grad school through their sex work. *Life is complicated*, Matthew thought, while recognizing, in the instant he thought it, just how banal a thought it was.

"Sit anywhere you like, darlin'," said a pert, mini-skirted waitress as she passed by with a tray of beers. Noticing, out of the corner of his eye, that John was on the left side of the room, Matthew chose a table on the right. A minute later the waitress was back.

"What'll you have, sweetheart?" she said.

"I'll have a Guinness, please," said Matthew. "But just a half-pint for now."

"You'll be flying on just the one wing," she said, smiling, and flitted away. Matthew watched her go, recognizing, in that instant, an old familiar ache. Yes, part of it was sexual, but the bigger part was loneliness. He was the brother of every man in that bar. He watched the dancer on the stage, now down to nothing at all. He glanced over at the nearest table with a dancer: the customer was leaning forward, his head as close as he could possibly get to the woman's pubis, as if he could somehow drink in her youth and vitality with his eyes. *Jesus*, Matthew thought, *we're pathetic. We're so pathetic.*

His reverie was interrupted by a striking blonde woman, dressed in a tiny black bikini and high heels. "Can I interest you in a dance?" she said.

CHAPTER THIRTY-TWO

But it wasn't Hannah. She was, certainly, as beautiful as Hannah, but this woman was a little taller, a little more buxom, and she spoke with an east European accent Matthew couldn't place more precisely. There was a bruise high up on her right thigh, and a small tattoo of a rose on her left ankle, and there was just a hint of hardness about her that was altogether absent from the photos Matthew had of Hannah. "I'd really like a dance," said Matthew.

"Back in a moment," said the blonde, and she sashayed away from his table, said something in passing to another girl—who laughed—then went to the bar. She picked up a box from behind the bar, then came back and sat at Matthew's table. "I'm Phoenix," she said, holding out her hand for him to shake.

"I'm Matthew. It's a pleasure to meet you."

"Are you visiting Salisbury?"

"Yes," said Matthew. "I'm here for just a few days." At that moment his waitress returned with his beer. "May I buy you a drink?" he asked Phoenix.

"Are you just having the one dance?"

"Yes, I think so. For now."

"Then no, thank you." Matthew's waitress left. "I'll just wait for a new song to come on," said Phoenix.

"I have a question for you," said Matthew. "The last time I was here I had a dance and a nice chat with another lovely blonde girl—a Canadian. Would you know if she's working today?"

"That would be Star," said Phoenix. "This is her day off. Come back tomorrow if you want to see her again."

"Thank you," said Matthew.

"And if you're really good," Phoenix added, "maybe the two of us will dance for you together."

"I'll remember that," said Matthew. The song that had been playing ended, and Phoenix got up, removed her bikini top and bottom, and climbed up on the box. For the first two minutes of the song she moved in such a way that Matthew saw every inch of her lower body, and in the last thirty seconds she crouched down, put her hands on his shoulders, and brought her breasts right up to his face, then moved them from side-to-side so her nipples brushed his lips. Matthew was left highly aroused. "What—what do I owe you?" he asked huskily as she slipped back into her bikini.

"Twenty pounds," she said, adjusting her bikini straps. "But Matthew, there's something else you should remember."

"What's that?" asked Matthew, handing her a twenty-pound note.

She brought her face down level with his ear, tickling it with her cinnamon-scented breath. "We have a back room," she said, "and there are rooms downstairs, too. And we know how to make a man feel like a man." She kissed his cheek, picked up her box, and strutted back towards the bar.

Matthew had to wait a couple of minutes to stand up. When he did, he left a ten-pound note for the beer on the table, then went outside into the sun.

★ ★ ★

By pre-arrangement, Matthew and John met on a bench in Salisbury's central square. John had just opened a newspaper when Matthew arrived. "No joy?" John asked.

"Her day off," said Matthew. "She's in tomorrow. Can you go again?"

"How am I going to explain this to my wife?" said John—but he was joking. "Sure," he said. "You arrive first this time. I'll follow." He folded up his paper.

"Two o'clock for me?" said Matthew.

"2:10 for me, then," said John. "And I'll buy a dance immediately. Hold off on speaking to Hannah until I've done that."

"Okay," said Matthew. "Are you free for dinner?"

"I'm not," said John, "but you can buy me a late lunch." They stood up, but as they moved forward a skate-boarder swept by them out of nowhere, ripping John's newspaper out of his hands as he did so. "What the—" said John.

"Shall we go after him?" asked Matthew.

"No," said John, "just a newspaper. Not worth risking a heart attack." They stood and watched the boy disappear behind a group of people on the square. "Perhaps he wants to catch up on Brexit," he added—then laughed.

Matthew said nothing, but he had the sense that he had just received another warning, and he was quiet as they made their way to a bistro a couple of streets away.

Chapter Thirty-Three

After lunch, Matthew had a decision to make. He'd seen what he wanted to see of Stonehenge in the three hours he'd spent there, which meant that he could either return to Salisbury Cathedral, visit Old Sarum, or wander Salisbury. For that matter, he could go back to his bed-and-breakfast and nap—though that seemed an unimaginative way of spending time in a county as beautiful and rich in history as Wiltshire. He opted for a new adventure, and hailed a cab.

"Can you tell me anything about Old Sarum?" he asked his driver.

The young man shrugged. "It's old," he said. "I don't know much about history, to be honest. I'm more into football."

Matthew nodded and said nothing. He knew a little more than his driver, but, admittedly, not much more. He'd read that Old Sarum was a prehistoric settlement, and that a fort had been built there during the Iron Age, probably because its location on the top of a hill made it relatively easy to defend. He knew that the Romans used it, and subsequently the Saxons, and then the Normans, and that the Normans had also built a cathedral there. He knew that arguments between two medieval power-brokers had eventually led to the decision to build a cathedral on the plain, and that, not surprisingly, a new town, Salisbury, had grown up around it, leading to the decline and eventual abandonment of the older settlement.

His cab dropped him off in the parking lot, and Matthew took a path leading to a bridge over the dry moat surrounding the hill-top fort. Before crossing, he looked back and admired the sight of Salisbury, and of the spire of the cathedral. As he crossed the bridge, a fighter jet aircraft streaked across the sky. It was beginning to cloud over.

He knew from a brochure at his B&B that the only part of the site he had to pay to visit was the ruins of the fort. He did not begrudge the expenditure, and spent an interesting half hour roaming the grassy ruins before descending a steep slope into the dry moat. Then he clambered back up again to visit the exposed foundations of the old, abandoned cathedral. He tried to imagine what the building would have been like. It occurred to him that whatever its advantages, this would have been a windy place at times. Indeed, the winds were beginning to buffet him a little as he continued his walk.

Undeterred, he descended into the moat again, then climbed back up the slope to the walls of the hilltop fort—which left him out of breath. He walked around the walls, having to brace himself now as the winds intensified, and he found himself thinking powerfully of his wife. *Grace*, he thought, *what could we have built together, you and me? What sort of a life could we have made?* And his thoughts strayed, inevitably, to the children they could have had, should have had—and he was overwhelmed, suddenly, by a terrible grief, a crushing sense of loss, and he sobbed, violently, as the winds grew stronger and it suddenly started to pour torrents of rain.

He completed his walk with some difficulty, climbing down from the wall when he drew close to the bridge. The rain was merciless now, and the winds were whistling and howling, and Matthew was soaked through and thoroughly miserable. He made his way to the on-site gift shop, stepped inside, and fumbled for his phone to call for a taxi. The gentleman behind the counter, seeing his condition, rummaged around for a moment then offered him a dry towel—ugly but clean. "The rain comes on very quickly up here sometimes," he said. "You might want to wait a few minutes 'til it lets up."

Matthew took his advice, and also took the opportunity to buy some postcards and a guide book. When the rain stopped, he phoned for a cab, bade the gentleman farewell, and walked out into a wetter and cooler world.

There was a woman standing on the fort side of the bridge, and when he came up to her, she turned, smiled, and wordlessly handed him a paper cup of sweet, hot tea. It was the gypsy woman from the cathedral. She took his arm and walked him to the car park, and waited with him there until his taxi arrived. And in the moment, it did not seem strange at all.

CHAPTER THIRTY-FOUR

Matthew finished the Pagels book in a hot bath, then put on his last clean clothes and went in search of Alia downstairs. He found her doing a crossword in her front sitting-room. "Could you recommend a good laundromat?" he asked her.

"There's the Wash Monster on Tompkins street," she replied, "I often take big loads there. Shall I write down the directions for you?"

"No need, thank you," said Matthew. "I'll look it up on my phone."

"Would you like a cup of tea before you go? I was just going to make one for myself," Alia said, putting her crossword puzzle aside.

"That would be very nice," said Matthew, grateful more for the possibility of friendly conversation than for the beverage itself—though it turned out that Alia made a fine cup of tea, and served digestive biscuits as well. They sat and talked for a while, and Matthew told her about visiting Old Sarum, while not mentioning his visit to Busy Bodies. "I was surprised there was so little left of the old cathedral," he told her. "Just the foundations."

"I can tell you why," she said. "When they built Salisbury Cathedral, they used stones from the old cathedral and other buildings on the hill. They just carted them down here."

"An early example of recycling," said Matthew.

"Exactly," said Alia. "Waste not, want not." She poured second cups of tea.

At the Wash Monster, Matthew caught up on his email. He sent Sharon and Andrew separate accounts of the last day-and-a-half. His email to Andrew was a difficult one: he had a responsibility to report that he had real hopes of seeing Hannah the next day, but he was reluctant to reveal that she might be an enslaved sex-worker;

he suspected that if he learned *that*, Andrew would catch the next flight over and put himself at risk of criminal prosecution if what he discovered led him to assault someone. His email to Sharon, on the other hand, was fairly detailed, though he realized, on rereading it, that he had said nothing about the bright-eyed old man or the gypsy-woman. He pressed *send*, leaned back, and reflected that whenever we tell a story, what we leave out may reveal as much about ourselves as what we tell.

Two minutes after emailing Sharon his phone pinged and he opened an excited email from Andrew: *This is amazing news! Thank you! Where is she? Is she okay? Has someone you know spoken with her? Do you have a photo of her you could send me? Please call me as soon as you've spoken with her—and put her on the phone if you possibly can!*

As an afterthought, perhaps, Andrew had attached a photo of his latest Edwin Long-style preparatory sketch for a painting: this one showed a row of three crosses, Jesus of Nazareth in the middle, with Roman soldiers off to one side throwing dice. Two figures were at the base of Jesus's cross gazing up at him—a man in his late twenties or early thirties, standing, and a middle-aged woman kneeling and holding her arms outstretched as if she would, if she could, clasp her son to her breast and heal him with the power of her love. *If only*, Matthew thought, *if only the world worked that way*. He found himself profoundly moved for the second time that day. He did not reply to Andrew's email. He needed to think carefully about what more he could say.

On his way back to Alia's bed-and-breakfast he stopped off in a bookshop and picked up a thriller, There wasn't a lineup so he chatted briefly with the cashier, then went back out into the streets of Salisbury, stopping just once more to buy a sandwich for his evening meal. He devoted his evening to reading, though he did also turn on the BBC radio news at 9:00, and fell asleep shortly afterwards, thinking, as he drifted off, that if Brexit were a game of soccer, the British team would be spectacularly successful at scoring own-goals.

He swam back into a kind of consciousness in the dream world whose light and temperature and *feel* he now recognized—and he was suddenly able to understand, in his dream-state, a connection he had hitherto failed to make in his waking life. *This* was the world Andrew painted in the style of Edwin Long. Or, possibly, this was the world for which Andrew's sketches served as a sort of imaginative portal. He was at the scene of the crucifixion. He was farther back than the vantage point of Andrew's painting, but, yes, that's where he was. He could see the three crosses with their tortured, twisted burdens. He could see the two figures at the base of Jesus's cross. He could see, not far from those figures, four Roman soldiers throwing dice. But between him and the small hill on which this grim scene played out was an expanse of well-trodden grass, sections worn away here and there; and immediately in front of him, and in front of a good many other people with whom he now stood shoulder-to-shoulder, was a line of Roman soldiers—their faces a multicultural reflection of the many countries the empire had conquered and occupied. And among those soldiers, most of whom looked bored, unsmiling, detached, he could see, very clearly, the broad-shouldered young man, and the East Asian teen, their mocking faces not at all obscured by their plain brass helmets.

The crowd around and behind Matthew had disparate elements. Some were quietly weeping; others, he sensed, were seething. There was no rejoicing, not here, at the grotesque suffering on show. Someone pushed him from behind, whether by accident or design, and as Matthew recovered from stumbling forward, his eyes met those of the two men he recognized. The broad-shouldered man recognized him in that same instant, his face registering both shock and, perversely, delight. He broke ranks with the other soldiers, drew his sword from its scabbard, and raised it to strike. Just before he could do so, however, a voice barked out a sharp order—*"Prohibere! Recede!"*—and the soldier froze, re-sheathed his sword, and sulkily stepped back into line.

Matthew's eyes flicked to the man who had given the order. It was a *decanus*, and a significantly older man than the soldiers he commanded, but he held himself erect and his voice was clear and authoritative. And he had piercing, bright blue eyes.

CHAPTER THIRTY-FIVE

B ut the dream was not over. As Matthew and the crowd stood bearing witness to the judicial murder unfolding in front of them, the sky began to cloud over, just as it had at Old Sarum, and the wind freshened, and dust began to whirl on the hill. Several minutes passed, and then a further natural provocation: there was a rumbling noise, and a moment later the earth shook. *Earthquake!* Matthew thought, and the voices that spoke out behind and beside him were almost certainly saying the same thing. It was not a major quake—it didn't last long—but it was enough to unsettle people even more, and when the shaking ceased many in the crowd started to leave. The soldiers, for their part, remained in line, but they looked ill at ease.

A stentorian voice from some distance away bellowed an order, and the soldiers snapped to attention. The *decanus* followed this up with a command of his own, and those soldiers who were carrying spears lowered them from the vertical to point into the crowd. At another order, they all took one measured step forward. The crowd took the hint. Matthew glanced back and saw that those behind him were melting away, most of them, and when the soldiers took another step forward, Matthew commenced his own retreat—first backing up, and then turning to run. The soldiers did not give chase; their leaders' intention had been simply to clear the area. Here and there small groups of people did stop running and turned again to look at the scene, but their numbers were radically reduced. They posed no threat to imperial authority.

Matthew stopped, too, and stood alone near the base of the hill. He did not know what to do. He did not know where to go. He looked at his hands. He looked at his feet. He was, he thought, fully conscious; he had agency; he could, if he wished, go back up the hill. He could scream. He could, if he chose, run at the soldiers. It would change nothing. Nothing. This particular die was cast.

And so Matthew awoke without physical trauma—without a blow to his head or a spear in his ribs. He opened his eyes and stared at the ceiling of his bedroom. He felt a great emptiness and, lurking at the edge of that emptiness, a dread about what might happen the next day.

★ ★ ★

At breakfast Matthew discovered, with some relief, that the Malcoviches had moved on. In their place was another single man—though a rather more presentable specimen than Matthew. Tall, blonde, handsome, and dressed entirely in black, the guest introduced himself as Baron. "It's a pleasure to meet you, Matthew," said Baron. "Alia tells me that you're now an expert on where to visit in Salisbury."

Matthew was startled by this, but then realized that his fellow guest was joking. "Well, I've certainly got around in the last couple of days," he said. "But no, I'm not an expert. Just an engaged tourist."

"I'm just in from the States," said Baron, "and I've wanted to see the cathedral and Stonehenge for years and years. Please tell me that you weren't disappointed."

"No, I wasn't disappointed at all," said Matthew. "I've had a very lively forty-eight hours."

They chatted for some time over the meal, and though Matthew's experience with Savio had taught him to be cautious about positive first impressions, he was charmed by Baron's warmth and enthusiasm. And, yes, Savio had seemed enthusiastic too, but Baron's enthusiasm struck him as deeply rooted, genuine, real. *But be careful*, Matthew thought. *Be very careful*.

"Where are you going today?" asked Baron, spreading homemade jam on his croissant with evident relish.

"I think I'll go back to the cathedral this morning," said Matthew, hoping that Baron wouldn't ask about his afternoon plans.

"That's where I'm headed!" said Baron, "right after breakfast. Alia—this is delicious! The jam, the croissants, the cheese omelette! You are the ideal hostess!" Alia, who had just come in, beamed.

"Why don't we walk together, then?" said Matthew. "The sun is shining now, but it could well cloud over this afternoon."

"Splendid!" said Baron. "Let's do it!" He got to his feet, stretched, and exclaimed: "Oh, and I must remember to buy a postcard to send to my godmother! She's an Anglican minister, and she'll be so jealous that I'm going to see the cathedral!"

CHAPTER THIRTY-SIX

It beggared belief that Clara should be Baron's godmother, but so it proved. And as Baron excitedly explained the familial connections that had made his spiritual guardianship possible, Matthew saw that Clara had roots in places other than Ontario. "I don't see her as much as I'd like," Baron said as they turned onto High Street, "but we often talk."

"Where do you live now?" asked Matthew, listening carefully to Baron, but also scanning the street for skateboarders.

"I'm in the music industry," said Baron, "so I travel a lot— I mean, *a lot*. I was most recently in New York, but I also spend time in Los Angeles, Vancouver, Toronto and Montreal. My group is interested in forging stronger links with the British industry, so that's why I'm over here. And when I knew I'd be coming over, I promised myself I'd visit Salisbury!"

"This is the High Street Gate," said Matthew pointing at the turreted archway as they approached it. "I think it's the main entry point into the Cathedral Close."

"I get such a kick out of these old structures," said Baron. "Think about what these things have withstood! Think about the people who have passed under here! History *fascinates* me!" They moved on, and a few minutes later the two men stood in front of the west face of the cathedral. "You know," said Baron, gazing up at it, "some people say that this doesn't compare with other cathedral fronts like the ones at Wells and Lincoln, but if that's true then I can't begin to imagine the beauty of those places."

"I wouldn't know," said Matthew, "but I think Salisbury is famous mostly for its spire and, of course, for the interior. It is . . . well. Words fail me."

"Can you imagine what it would have been like to work on this project?" said Baron. "To see the spire rise? Can you imagine?"

"Maybe some of our own ancestors did," said Matthew. "Our blood may be in these stones."

"I like that thought," said Baron. "I really like that thought."

They entered the Cathedral, and Matthew gave Baron space to make the same discoveries he had made—the beauty of the bronze baptismal font in the shape of a cross, water flowing gently from each of four spouts; the stained-glass windows—the most beautiful, perhaps, in the Trinity Chapel—some of their glass dating back to the 1260s, and the dark polished marble of the columns in the nave. They rendezvoused after Baron had seen the oldest clock in the world, and were just about to launch back into conversation when they were approached by a middle-aged male usher in a blazer. "Gentlemen," he said, "the choir is about to sing. Would you like to sit up with them?" "Would we! Yes!" said Baron. The usher led them up to the choir stalls, seating them there as a forty-person choir clad in surplices and stoles filed in, opened their scores, and, under the direction of a restrained but commanding conductor, began to sing. For the next hour the cathedral vibrated and rang with crystalline human voices and powerful organ music. Matthew and Baron were transfixed.

As the session was coming to an end, a formidably large man—nearly seven feet tall and conspicuously-muscled—advanced up the central aisle of the church toward the choristers. Everything about the way he moved implied a threat. When he reached about half way he stopped, hunched over, gripped his fists in front of his body, and howled. The sound was chilling—deep, guttural, angry. Matthew and Baron looked at each other, then both rose at the same moment and stepped into the choir aisle; they went to the top of the stairs leading to the choir stalls and stood there, sentinels between the choir and the howling giant. As they were doing this, several ushers moved toward the interloper from different directions—but he was not in the least deterred: he continued his guttural howling. When they reached him and tried to speak to him, he ignored them, and when they sought gently to lead him away, he shook them off easily—then moved once again toward Baron, Matthew and the choir.

Baron and Matthew had been joined, meanwhile, by several male choristers, while the rest of the choir—many of whom were women and children—were being shepherded out by a back way. "Let's get off the steps," said one of the choristers, so they all moved down, which meant that those who had joined Matthew and Baron could now fan out around them and present a half-circle wall to the advancing giant. In a couple of seconds he was almost to them, and Matthew crouched, rugby-style, preparing to launch himself forward—and most of the other men did the same. Matthew figured that if enough of them barreled into him at the same time, there was a chance that they could knock him to the ground and immobilize him.

At that moment, Baron spoke out authoritatively from the centre of the half-circle. "Go back. Go back! You are not wanted here."

The giant stopped howling, stopped advancing, stared malevolently at Baron. "What are you doing here, Barachiel?" he snarled.

Baron did not answer. He held his ground. The giant stood, swaying slightly, for a moment. He then turned his attention to Matthew. "Go home, Matthew, while you still can," he said, his voice preternaturally deep—a demonic rumble. "Go home."

"I'm staying here," said Matthew. He had no idea who this man was, or how he knew his name, but he had no intention of taking orders from him.

"Then you will pay the price," said the giant. And he laughed—a terrible, mocking, bone-chilling laugh. He turned and headed back down the aisle, leaving behind a feral scent and a large number of shaken choristers and tourists.

Chapter Thirty-Seven

Matthew and Baron left the cathedral and stopped in at the Café Diwali, a restaurant serving Indian street food in a bright conservatory. Matthew looked squarely at his new friend. "Baron," he said, "that giant fellow knew you—but he called you by a different name."

"You're right," said Baron. "He thinks he knows me."

"Is he wrong?"

"We've bumped into one another on previous occasions. And I suspect we'll bump into one another again." Baron reached into his pocket, took out a key, and turned it over and over between the fingers of his left hand.

"So why are you here? Did Clara send you?"

"No," said Baron, "but we do play on the same team, so to speak. I know why you're here, Matthew, and I'd like to help you—but I'm bound by certain constraints."

"Do you know that I'm going to a strip club this afternoon?" Matthew asked.

"No, I can't read your mind. I know you're looking for Hannah, and I know she's here in Salisbury." He held his key between the thumb and forefinger of his left hand, brought his right hand close, made a gesture—and the key bent.

Matthew raised his eyebrows, but stayed focused. "Well, then," he said, "let me tell you that I hope to meet her at a strip club called Busy Bodies later this afternoon. I'm going there at 2:00."

"Do you have anyone backing you up?" asked Baron.

"I have help from a British missing-persons investigator, John Deacon. He's coming to the club at 2:10."

Baron nodded. "It's good that you'll have a companion."

"Can you come, too?"

"Here's the problem," said Baron. "If I come, our giant-friend shows up, too. There's a kind of fearful symmetry at work here." He reached up and appeared to pluck another key out of the air, then brought that key down to the table and placed the two keys in opposition to each other. The first was tarnished and still bent. The second was shiny, straight, and new.

"That's a clever trick," said Matthew.

"In this game there are no tricks. And the stakes are fearfully high."

"I don't think I understand that," said Matthew.

"It's complex," said Baron. "Deeply complex." He met Matthew's eyes. "You are not alone, Matthew, but everything depends on what you do." The two keys vanished from the table.

★ ★ ★

Matthew entered Busy Bodies at two minutes after 2:00. He passed the same doorman/bouncer, and once again proceeded into the club room. Again, a topless woman was dancing on the stage, and again, there were a couple—no, three—women dancing on little boxes at tables occupied by a customer or two. Matthew returned to the table he had chosen on his previous visit. A couple of minutes later the same waitress came up to him. "Hey, handsome," she said. "Another tiny Guinness?"

"Yup," said Matthew. "And is Star here?"

"You had Phoenix yesterday," said the waitress, putting on a mock-severe tone.

"I had Star the time before that," said Matthew, doing his best to sound like a habitué of strip clubs.

"Let's hope Phoenix doesn't find out," said the waitress, and she flitted away. Matthew watched her out of the corner of his eye and saw her place his order with the bartender, then push open a door to the right of the bar and stick her head in. A moment later she re-emerged with a beautiful blonde young woman in a negligée and pointed towards him.

The young woman was Hannah. Matthew had found her. He felt two things simultaneously: a flush of satisfaction at making contact, and a sense of grief at the circumstances.

Hannah picked up one of the boxes and made her way between tables to him, saying something briefly to another man—who had probably asked for a dance—on route. She arrived at Matthew's table, smiled at him, put the box on the floor, and sat down. "I hear you might want a dance or two," she said.

"I would certainly like some of your time," said Matthew—and he extended his hand. "I'm Matthew."

"I'm Star," said Hannah, taking his hand. "But Cheryl said I'd danced for you before, and I don't remember you. I usually remember the handsome ones."

"No," said Matthew. "But you come highly recommended." He remembered suddenly John's saying that he should not speak with Hannah until he had arrived, and he bit his lip in self-reproach.

"Well, that's nice," said Hannah. "A girl likes to be appreciated. What can I do for you?"

"Let's start with a dance," said Matthew. "And then maybe we can go somewhere else."

"Oh, you'd like something a little special, would you? A little extra?" She smiled coyly. *Jesus*, Matthew thought, *how deeply is she into this? Are the drugs so powerful they can obliterate a person's whole sense of self in a matter of weeks? Or is there something more than drugs at work?*

At that instant he saw John enter the club, and see him. John frowned, but then wiped his face clear of expression and headed towards the table he'd sat at on his last visit. That one was occupied, as it happened, so he took the one nearest to it.

A song was ending, and Hannah got up to take off her negligée. "You know," said Matthew, "I think I'd like to go somewhere more private right now. If you don't mind."

Hannah looked at him. Matthew thought he saw a flicker of—what, reluctance? Anxiety? Fear? cross her face. "You sure you don't want a dance or two first, Cowboy?" she asked. "Your drink hasn't even arrived."

"I'd just really like to have some private time with you," said Matthew. "Sorry that you went to the trouble of bringing the box over."

"That's no problem," she said. "So this is how it works. I'm going to the bar to have a quick word with the bartender, then I'm going to take a moment or two to freshen up. In a couple of minutes he'll send someone over to look after the business details, then she'll bring you downstairs and we'll have ourselves a party. Does that sound good to you?"

"That sounds very good to me," said Matthew.

"Great. Here comes your drink, Cowboy. Why don't you have a mouthful or two and relax . . . before I help you relax some more?"

Hannah picked up her box, put a finger on the tip of Matthew's nose, then headed back across the bar. Matthew took out his wallet to pay for the beer Cheryl was about to set in front of him, but she stopped him: "Everything goes on the same bill," she said. "And don't you move quickly, Tiger? Usually the customers like to check out a girl's goods before they take her downstairs."

"I know what I like," said Matthew, playing a role he didn't feel altogether comfortable with.

"You sit tight and Madeleine will be over in just a minute," said Cheryl. She touched his shoulder as she turned to go, and for a second Matthew entertained the fantasy that she liked him, that she would sleep with him for free if he asked her to dinner, that she would marry him and leave off waitressing in a strip club. And then he reminded himself that she, like everyone else, was trained to make him feel good and all the readier to part with large sums of money. And he wondered whether he'd brought enough money to get himself alone with Hannah, and how he was going to persuade her to walk out of the club with him—or join him later, in secret, so he could get her out of the country.

CHAPTER THIRTY-EIGHT

Madeleine turned out to be another stunningly attractive young woman in her early thirties, but she wore a dress which, while short, might just have passed muster on a receptionist in a professional office. She took the seat Hannah had vacated, and smiled at Matthew. "Just a couple of questions," she said. "I won't make you wait long."

"Fire away," said Matthew.

Madeleine took her cell phone out of a tiny purse and placed it face-up on the table. "First, are you a member of any police force in the United Kingdom or Great Britain?" she asked. Matthew guessed that she was recording their conversation.

"No," said Matthew. "I'm not a police officer anywhere."

"And second," said Madeleine, "are you wearing or carrying any sort of recording device?"

"I have my cell phone with me," said Matthew, "but I don't intend using it."

"May I look after it for the next little while?" asked Madeleine, still smiling.

Matthew considered this. "Is that a pre-requisite for going downstairs?" he asked.

"It is for customers we don't yet know," she said. "When you become a regular customer, we no longer feel the need."

"Okay," said Matthew. He clicked the phone off, then handed it to her.

"I'll take good care of it," she said, slipping it into her purse. "And now, one final thing to attend to: we require a deposit of one thousand pounds. Cash."

"Out here in the open?" asked Matthew, looking around the room.

"No," she said. "We're going to go through that door over there," she pointed, "and when we enter the corridor, and before we go downstairs, you're going to give it to me."

"Okay," said Matthew again. "Does that cover everything?"

"That covers massage, oral, vaginal," said Madeleine. "Anything else, you negotiate with Star."

"Can I take her out on a date?" asked Matthew. "Can I take her out for dinner and back to my hotel room?"

"You negotiate that with her," said Madeleine. "But every now and then we get a client with bad intentions, so she would have to clear that with the boss. We'd need to know details."

"Are you the boss?" asked Matthew.

"No," said Madeleine. "The boss is scary. You don't want to meet the boss."

"Hey, I'm just here for a good time," said Matthew. "I like girls. Star is really sweet."

"She'll show you a good time," said Madeleine. "Would you like to finish your drink?"

Matthew downed a mouthful, then put the glass back on the table. "Let's go," he said.

★ ★ ★

Once through the door, Madeleine turned back to Matthew. Matthew counted ten one-hundred-pound notes into her hand. "I'm guessing there's no receipt," he said.

"Aren't you the wit," said Madeleine, tucking the money into her purse. "Come." They went down a long flight of stairs. The steps were broad, the walls painted an attractive off-white. There was a slender brass railing. They came to the bottom, and Matthew followed her along a short corridor, with closed doors on either side—and then another set of stairs.

"I'm surprised you don't have an elevator," said Matthew, negotiating these.

"Salisbury is an old city," said Madeleine, glancing back at him.

"Not by British standards, I should have thought," said Matthew. "We're already a good long way below the water table."

"They had to worry about air raids during the last war," said Madeleine. "They dug down pretty deep." They reached the bottom of this second set of stairs, and passed along another short corridor—again with closed doors on both sides.

"This doesn't feel like a bomb shelter," said Matthew.

"We've made a lot of renovations," said Madeleine. "This is the last flight." Again they descended. Matthew had the disorientating sense that they could now be almost anywhere, and that his cell phone wouldn't have worked even if she had left it with him. Going up again would be a real challenge for older men, he thought.

At the bottom of this third flight of stairs there was a remarkably spacious and carpeted lobby—a lobby that would have cost a king's ransom to build so far underground. In the lobby there was a well-equipped cleaning cart, side-by-side with a laundry cart filled with fluffy fresh towels, plush house coats, and folded satin sheets and pillow slips. There was, however, no cleaner in sight. There were three doors, spaced far apart, all of them closed—and there was also what looked suspiciously like an elevator. "There *is* an elevator," Matthew said.

"That's for when you come up," said Madeleine. "After you've had a nice shower. We like to loosen up your joints on the way down." She laughed. She led him to the last of the three doors, knocked lightly, then opened the door and stepped aside for Matthew to enter. He went through, and there, with her bare back facing him, but with a towel draped around her waist, was Hannah. Madeleine closed the door from outside.

Chapter Thirty-Nine

Except that it wasn't Hannah. It was the East Asian teenage boy—the skateboarder—wearing a blonde wig identical to Hannah's own hairstyle. He turned slowly, laughed mockingly at Matthew's expression, and dropped the towel to reveal that he was wearing nothing more than a leather jockstrap and fishnet stockings.

"Jesus Christ!" said Matthew. He took a step towards the boy. "Where is Star?" he demanded. There was a curtain next to the boy, and that curtain was suddenly drawn to reveal Savio Malise, seated, in an armchair with plush velvet armrests. His head was drooped to the left, his chin pointing down, but he was very much alive. He looked sideways at Matthew with a twisted smile.

"Matthew, we cross paths once more," he said. "I'm not going to say it's an absolute joy to see you again, but I confess that it gives me some satisfaction. Please forgive me not getting up: I have a bit of difficulty getting around these days, thanks to your little Mexican friend."

"You jumped me," said Matthew. "Don't look for any sympathy."

"Details, details," said Savio. "Don't be boring, Matthew." He turned to the boy in the jockstrap and stockings. "You may go, Struan," he said, "but don't go far. Who knows, we may find our friend has exotic tastes."

"Take a long, long hike," said Matthew, opening the door for the boy and watching him warily as he passed. He closed the door again.

"Now," said Savio, "let's you and I have a talk. A nice little chat." He intertwined his fingers. "What is it you want, Matthew?"

"You know damn well what I want," said Matthew. "I want Hannah Hutchinson released to me."

"Why?" asked Savio, his voice amused.

"Because she is the beloved fiancée of my client, and the beloved child of her parents," Matthew said.

"Are you sure that's the reason?" said Savio. "Really sure, Matthew? Be honest. Are you sure you didn't, shall we say, *fall in love* with her yourself? Are you sure you didn't feel a certain erotic . . . *anticipation* as you came down those stairs? Wasn't there just a tiny little sexual charge when you came through the door? I mean, she's adorable, isn't she, Matthew? What red-blooded man wouldn't want to just eat her up?"

"I'm here to free the girl from sexual enslavement," said Matthew, as calmly as he could manage, "and to return her to freedom and to the arms of my client, her fiancé. It's as simple as that. And I'll do what I have to do to make it happen."

"So noble," said Savio. "So admirable. A little *patriarchal*, perhaps, but that's neither here nor there. But Matthew," he added, "you assume that Andrew Greenshield will want her back when he finds out how she's been spending the last several weeks. She's damaged goods, you know. She's been *used* over and over again. And she doesn't complain, Matthew. I'd say she quite enjoys the lifestyle. I mean, it beats the hell out of living above a studio in an industrial warehouse and shopping for groceries at Metro."

Matthew replied through clenched teeth. "My client is a good man. He loves his fiancée, and wants her back, and I am here to make sure that happens."

"The thing you don't understand, Matthew," said Savio, "is that I don't really care what Mr. Greenshield wants. His desires don't interest me in the least. Give me a reason to surrender her to you. Bribe me. Make it worth my while."

"You should release her," said Matthew, "because she means nothing to you."

"But she *does*, Matthew," said Savio. "She means everything to me. I want her because Andrew wants her, and because her parents want her, and because you want her. Do you understand?

I want her because she is important to all of you. So there's that. Plus, I delight in degradation, Matthew, and I have degraded Hannah with great skill and subtlety."

"You're a right son-of-a-bitch, aren't you," said Matthew, his voice filled with contempt.

"Oh, you have no idea, Matthew," said Savio. "You don't know the least of it." He laughed. "But think for a moment, my friend, of the secret pleasure you've taken in your own small-scale voyeurisms, your violations of another's private moments, the true crime stories in the magazines you read, the bombing of people from cultures you don't like. That's the shadow in you, Matthew—the pathetically small, dirty little shadow. The shadow that's ashamed of itself." He suddenly righted his head, stretched his neck, got to his feet.

"What—" Matthew began.

"I am *the* Shadow," said Savio. "I'm the original. Unashamed. Unrepentant. So tell me . . . what can you offer me for this insignificant girl? This little *slut* that I rescued from the whirlpool, and whose life belongs to me. This *juicy* little plaything of mine."

Matthew was reduced to silence. Nothing in his life had prepared him for this. Evil deeds he had encountered before, in all sorts of incarnations and variations—but articulate, conscious, embodied Evil was a whole different thing. "What are you?" he asked finally.

"I've told you," said Savio. "You need to listen more carefully. You need to pay attention, Matthew. Now, make *me* an offer."

"What do *you* want?" Matthew managed.

Savio stared at him. "What do I want? That's a good question. That's the right question." He moved to Matthew and put his left index finger on his chest, just above his heart. "Is she worth a year off your life, Matthew? Hmm? Understand that you might not have a year left, so you may be choosing oblivion. I know that you're a religious man, Matthew—a pathetic, laughable thing, all in itself—but are you willing to place a wager that there is something more to come, that *this* isn't it? Are you willing to give me twelve months off your own life here and now in return for temporary custody of another man's little trollop?"

Matthew stared at Savio. He suspected, he intuited, he all-but-knew that this was a deal Savio had the power to deliver on and to enforce. He didn't know how—he didn't know what infernal mechanism might be at work—but he believed, in his gut and in his soul, that he would be making a bargain to which he would be bound. And so he thought, briefly but deeply, of the quality of his life: the wife-sized hole that Grace's death had left; the absence of children; the dearth of truly deep friendships; his feeble, struggling faith. "Yes," he said. "I am."

CHAPTER FORTY

"Well, well, well," said Savio. "What an interesting choice. What a *brave* choice, Matthew, if I may say so. And look—you're still alive! You could have years and years left. Or, of course, you could have just days . . . and if so you've surrendered the chance to do anything meaningful with what remains of your oh-so-precious life."

"Yes, I get it. Thank you for the clarification."

Savio turned. "Come," he said, and Matthew followed him. As soon as he passed the curtain, which had not been drawn completely, he saw that the space opened up into a large bedroom. There was a king-sized bed against the wall, and on that bed, clad in her negligée still, was Hannah—fast asleep, or, perhaps, drugged. "There's your prize," said Savio. "Shake her awake. Carry her off on your white horse. She's all yours."

Matthew moved to the bed. "Where are her clothes?" he asked.

"Mmm," said Savio. "And that raises a question, doesn't it? Who will get her dressed? Why not tarry an hour, Matthew? Surely, she owes you an hour's entertainment for the salvation you've given her? Enjoy her for a single hour. One more man won't make any difference."

Matthew took a deep breath. "Where are her clothes?" he repeated.

"Fool," said Savio. "There's a wardrobe over there." He gestured. "She can take what she wants. But at least undress her, Matthew. You owe yourself a little something."

"Get out," said Matthew.

Savio moved toward the door, then turned and looked at him. "You realize you haven't seen the last of me, Matthew?" he said. "I collect on all my bets."

"I gave you a year off my life—not my soul," said Matthew.

"True," said Savio. "But I like to make an appearance when time's up. Just to rub it in."

"Great," said Matthew. "See you then."

"Or maybe earlier," said Savio. "One never knows. At least—*you* won't."

"Get the fuck out," said Matthew. Savio left, leaving behind the same feral scent that the giant had left in Salisbury Cathedral. Matthew shook his head, went to the wardrobe, opened it, and chose a green dress that looked as though it wouldn't raise eyebrows on the streets of Salisbury—or, for that matter, Toronto. He took it to the bed, placed it beside Hannah, and, on a whim, opened the drawer of the bedside table. Inside the drawer was a woman's wallet, a small make-up kit, and, wonder-of-wonders, a Canadian passport. Matthew opened it. It was Hannah's.

He gently shook her awake. When her eyes opened, she looked at him with bewilderment—then looked around the room. Her eyes closed, and she took a deep, shuddering breath. "Where am I?" she said.

"You're in Salisbury," said Matthew.

"I remember," she said. "I remember. God help me, I remember."

"Do you remember the wave? The wave that swept you off the whaling boat?"

A pause. "Yes."

"Do you remember being in Mexico?"

A longer pause. "Yes."

"Do you remember that this is the basement of a club called Busy Bodies?"

She closed her eyes, and her face convulsed in pain. "Yes."

"Okay," said Matthew. "It's over. I've come to take you home."

"Who are you?" She opened her eyes again.

"My name is Matthew. I'm a private investigator. Andrew hired me."

"Where is Andrew? Is he here? Are my parents here?" She sat up.

"No," said Matthew. "I'll take you to them. I'm going to sit in a chair behind that curtain while you get dressed, then we'll leave together."

★ ★ ★

Once Hannah was dressed, she and Matthew left the room and summoned the elevator. They rode it in silence. When the doors opened, Madeleine was waiting for them. "Well, hello," she said.

"Madeleine," said Matthew. Hannah did not speak.

"Your cell phone," said Madeleine, handing it to him. "A severance cheque for you, sweetie," she extended an envelope to Hannah. Hannah did not take it.

Matthew took it and tucked it into his jacket pocket. "Evidence," he said to Hannah. And to Madeleine: "Anything else?"

"A friendly word to the wise," said Madeleine, addressing Hannah: "Get an STD test before having relations with anyone you care about." She paused, then added gently. "I don't mean that in a cruel way. It's just sensible." Hannah teared up; Matthew took her elbow and steered her down the hall.

John was waiting in the lobby. "They told me you were coming out," he said, approaching them. "They sussed out that we were together."

"Hannah, this is John," said Matthew. "He's a friend." Hannah nodded tightly. "I'll fill you in later, John," Matthew added. "This operation is more sinister than it seems."

"I don't doubt that," said John.

Chapter Forty-One

On the flight home, fortified by a coffee, Hannah turned to Matthew. "How do I explain what happened to me?" she asked. "Because I don't know the answer. I don't know how I got from New Brunswick to Mexico. I don't know how I got to England. I mean, I remember bits and pieces, but it's as if I'm remembering a dream. I'm not sure what's real. I don't know what I was thinking. I don't know who I was."

"You have amnesia," said Matthew. "That makes perfect sense to me."

"I must tell Andrew what I do remember."

"I'll leave that to you," said Matthew. "My mandate from Andrew was to find you. Bringing you home is a happy bonus. What you tell him is between the two of you."

"Thank you," she said quietly.

"You're welcome," he replied.

Andrew, Hannah's friend Rebecca, and Hannah's parents were waiting in the arrivals. There were tears, hugs, more thanks. "What do I owe you?" asked Andrew, drawing Matthew aside for a moment.

"The $10,000 is pretty well gone," said Matthew. "Last minute flights are expensive. There's about $400 left. And that's all I need."

"That seems absurdly cheap," said Andrew.

"I saw some interesting places, and I had some good meals," said Matthew. "I'm content. I wish you both joy. She's a lovely lady." They shook hands—a handshake that turned into a hug.

Matthew and Sharon had exchanged a number of emails while he was at Heathrow Airport, and Sharon had agreed to pick him up just outside the terminal at Pearson International. Matthew was surprised that his texts went unanswered. He called her, and her message clicked on. He called the office and, again, the message machine answered. Matthew deliberated for a moment, then called Dr. Barker's office.

"Marika, have you seen Sharon?" Matthew asked. "She was going to pick me up at the airport, but she isn't answering her cell or the office phone."

"She dropped in at 10:30 to see if she could get me a muffin," said Marika, "and she told me she was picking you up. I haven't seen her since then."

"Well, that's a little odd," said Matthew. "Thank you. See you soon."

"I'll tell her to get in touch if I hear from her," said Marika, her voice troubled.

Matthew spent the twenty-five minutes on the airport train worrying. It was not like Sharon to fall out of touch. Could her phone have lost its charge? Not for this length of time: she always carried a charger. Could her phone have been lost or stolen? That was possible, certainly, but it wouldn't have prevented her calling from a public phone and leaving a message. Sharon might be fond of gossip sites on the internet, but she was a well-organized and responsible employee. And it certainly wouldn't have explained her not being at the airport.

Arriving at Union, Matthew ordered an Uber. The driver took him to his office, which Matthew found locked—appropriately enough, given Sharon's absence. Nothing was out of place. There were no signs of a hasty departure. But there was also no used coffee cup in the recycling bin. He had the driver take him home.

He knew something was wrong there as soon as he unlocked the door. Mr. Smudge rarely failed to greet him, but he wasn't waiting at the door this time. "Mr. Smudge!" Matthew called. "Smudgie!" He checked every room in the condo—checked under the bed—checked the balcony. No cat. The litter box looked as though it had been cleaned recently, which meant . . . well, what did it mean? That Mr. Smudge had been gone several days? Or that he had been taken from home sometime in the last six hours or so? The lowered level of the bottle of rye suggested that Steven had made several visits, so that might mean that Mr. Smudge's departure was recent. Could Steven have taken him to the vet?

Matthew called Steven. "He's not there?" said Steven. "He was there at breakfast. We had a great visit. Has someone broken in?"

"There's no evidence of that," said Matthew, "and if they have, they locked the door from the outside."

"Could they have come in through the balcony?"

"The balcony door was locked," said Matthew. "And the windows, too. If you still have your key, someone else has one, too."

"Let me check," said Steven. But he did have his key.

Matthew' pressing concern was for Sharon's safety. He had a number for her mother, but remembered Sharon saying that she was a volatile woman, given to manic highs and suicidal lows. He called a friend in the police department, Al Smith, and asked if anyone answering to Sharon's description had been injured or killed in a traffic accident in the last few hours. The answer was no. "Any other Jane Does in their early thirties?" he asked. Again, no.

"Should we put out a missing persons bulletin?" asked Inspector Smith.

"If she doesn't turn up by tomorrow morning, I'll call you back," said Matthew. "But can I ask you to keep a close eye on reports?"

"Of course," said Al. "Is this your Sharon, Matt?"

"Yes. It is," said Matthew. He hung up, sat back in his chair, thought about that. *His* Sharon. Well, yes. Not a wife. Not a daughter. Not a lover. But maybe the closest thing he had to a meaningful relationship with a woman. Six years in harness together. Did he care about her? Yes, of course he did. Did he trust her? Absolutely. He massaged his scalp.

Call a locksmith, he said to himself, and found an online listing. To his surprise, a Mr. Cole said he could be there in two hours. Matthew prepared himself a simple dinner from the contents of his fridge and cupboards, and ate it while catching up on the news with one of several newspapers that had accumulated during his absence. Steven had brought them inside.

The locksmith arrived at 7:00 p.m. and finished the job in an hour. He was a friendly fellow and would have enjoyed chatting while he worked, but Matthew wasn't in the right frame of mind. He called Al Smith again, but he had no news. Matthew thanked him, then decided to visit the work-out room. Forty-five minutes on the treadmill calmed him a little, and a hot bath helped more, but his anxiety about Sharon and Mr. Smudge returned when he went to bed. He lay staring at the ceiling and mapping out a plan of action for the morning. Midnight came and went without sleep, so he made himself a mug of hot cocoa, and swallowed a sleeping pill.

He was woken up at 3:00 a.m. by a call to his phone. "Matthew," said the lightly-accented voice—the same voice that had called him to say *Maybe next time* the previous week—"if you want to see Sharon, you need to take a little road trip."

"Where?" asked Matthew. And then "Where!" when the voice was slow to respond.

"Peterborough," said the caller. "Ninety minutes from where you are at this time of night. Take a room at the Holiday Inn. I'll call you there."

Matthew repacked his suitcase, and was in a cab to the bus terminal thirty minutes later. At the last moment he slipped a street knife, a shiv, into his pocket.

Chapter Forty-Two

If the young man at the front desk of the Holiday Inn was surprised to see Matthew at 5:25 a.m. he didn't show it. "Do you have a reservation, sir?" he said and, upon learning that Matthew didn't, he asked if he had any preference in room type and location, and gave him a double overlooking the Otonabee River. "Breakfast service starts at 6:00, sir," he added.

Matthew found his room, hung up his shirts, checked the wi-fi, then laid down on the bed. He'd brought the thriller he'd purchased in Salisbury with him, but he didn't feel like reading. Espionage derring-do paled beside the rigours of real life.

At 7:00 he went down to breakfast, taking his phone with him. Sharon's disappearance had to be somehow connected to Savio Malise and his crew—didn't it? Or was that too simplistic, too obvious? He remembered something that the blue-eyed old man had said at Stonehenge—that help would "come from different places and draw on very different sources of strength." If that were true of *help*, might it not also be true of *threats*? He could not be sure, but he suspected that Clara and Baron, on the one hand, and the blue-eyed old man and the gypsy-woman on the other, were from different places, different circles. Might it not also be possible that the giant and the broad-shouldered young man were similarly from different spheres? Was it possible that the whole situation was like the Syrian Civil War, with the Syrian government in one corner, the self-styled Jihadis in another, Sunni rebel groups here, Kurdish liberation forces there, and the Americans, Russians, Iranians and Israelis swooping in from the sidelines? And if that were true, who—or what—was Savio Malise? Was he in fact the Devil, as he had seemed to style himself? Or was he just another bit player, albeit one with delusions of demonic grandeur, because, surely, the Father of Lies, if there were any such thing, would not need to boast about it. Or perhaps the Father of Lies *did* need to boast, because narcissism was written into his Satanic DNA. In any event, Matthew went down to breakfast, pausing only, halfway there, to send a text message to Al Smith, telling him where he was and why he was there.

His waitress was in her late twenties, warm, personable, and, he guessed, from a rural community. "Coffee or tea, sir?" she asked, handing him a menu. Her nametag said *Maureen.*

Matthew ordered coffee. He'd had very little sleep, after all.

"Would youse like milk or cream?"

"Um, cream. Please." She bustled away.

The call came as he was finishing his omelette. "Tell your cab driver to take you to the old Peter Robinson College. Go behind the residences, onto the Greenway Trail. Someone will be waiting for you."

"Now?" said Matthew.

"Now."

Matthew called a cab from his table, signalling Maureen at the same time. He paid his bill with cash, tipping her generously. "Thanks, Hon. Come again," she said. He went back into the lobby, past the front desk, and through the main doors. His cab was there two minutes later.

"Peter Robinson College," he said to the grizzled veteran behind the wheel.

"Jesus, that don't exist no more," said his driver. "They closed that."

"Are the buildings still there?"

"Oh, yeah, the buildings are still there." The driver eased out onto George Street. "Used to be part of Trent University. That's where all the queers and artist-types hung out."

"Why did they close it?"

"Beats me. They shoulda got rid of the queers, too."

"Nothing wrong with queers," said Matthew, feeling he should say something.

"No offence intended," said the driver.

"None taken," said Matthew. He looked out the window. What he had seen of the city was fairly attractive, and he could easily imagine himself living there.

They arrived at the site of the former Peter Robinson College and Matthew took note of what he suspected had once been low-rise student residences, now town houses for rent, then walked across the campus, threading his way between a couple of buildings. He came eventually to a trail, and there, waiting for him, inevitably, were the broad-shouldered man and the East Asian teen.

"It's like a weird class reunion," said Matthew. "Where's Sharon?"

"We'll take you to her," said the teen. He went off the trail and began scuffling with his feet in the grasses, weeds, and wildflowers. He apparently found what he was seeking, because he bent down and lifted something. It was, Matthew saw, a sort of cover made from interwoven sticks and twigs—close enough together that the construction looked reasonably solid, but with enough room here and there for small plugs of sod with vegetative matter to form a camouflage. Underneath that was something resembling a manhole cover, and the broad-shouldered man moved forward, twisted it, then pulled it open. "After you," said the teen, bowing theatrically.

"Nope," said Matthew. "After you. I don't jump people from behind. You do." The two stared at him for a moment, then one after the other climbed into the opening. Matthew tapped the pocket with his knife, cursed under his breath, then climbed in after them.

CHAPTER FORTY-THREE

They were in a passage-way—a kind of tunnel even narrower than the one at Monte Alban, though, mercifully, higher. It was not well-illuminated, but there was a lighting system built into the roof: enough light that Matthew could keep tabs on his two escorts. The broad-shouldered one turned a crank built into the wall, and the hole through which they'd entered was sealed. He and his fellow-thug then struck out along the passage, with Matthew on their heels. Matthew figured he might as well name them, at least for his own amusement, so in the privacy of his mind he labelled the teen 'Dick' and the broad-shouldered man 'Harry.'

When Matthew had arrived at Peter Robinson, he'd noticed that it occupied a small flat area before the land began to rise into a steep hill. It was easy to get disorientated underground, but by his rough reckoning they were now walking straight into the belly of that hill. The tunnel didn't slope down much, but it did-n't need to for them to have a greater and greater mass on top of them. He found the thought a little oppressive, especially given the nature of his company. If he died down here, he would already be buried deep below this part of the city.

Any lightness, any optimism, any hope that Matthew might have had for a happy resolution to these proceedings died when they came to a black door in the tunnel. Harry opened it, stepped to one side, and turned to see Matthew's reaction at the sight of his cat, Mr. Smudge, hanging lifeless from a length of fishing line.

"You bastards," said Matthew. "You fucking bastards." Dick laughed, then he and Harry walked on, moving their heads side-ways to avoid bumping into the poor, dead cat. Matthew stopped in front of Mr. Smudge, put his hand on his back and stroked him. Then he too walked on, suppressing tears by biting down on his tongue until it bled. Mr. Smudge had been more dog than cat—emotionally needy, affectionate, happiest in human laps. If he ever had the opportunity to grieve, Matthew knew he would grieve him deeply.

More passage. One more door. But Dick and Harry approached this door differently. They stopped, looked at one another, then Dick knocked. A moment's pause, then the unmistakeable sound of Savio Malise's voice, echoing from within: "Come." Dick opened the door, he and Harry entered and fanned out to either side, and Matthew followed them in.

CHAPTER FORTY-FOUR

Savio stood in the middle of a large open space, which, Matthew realized, was almost certainly a cave rather than something engineered by humans. But in the very centre of that space someone had set up a structure that looked like a cross between a cage and a wrestling ring. In fact, Matthew saw, that was precisely what it was: the kind of space in which Mixed Martial Arts fighters fought their battles.

"Our third and final meeting, Matthew," said Savio. "I'm collecting on your debt."

"Where is Sharon?" asked Matthew.

Savio pointed up at the roof of the cave, and a light flicked on illuminating its deeper recesses. There, at the top, was a motionless figure dangling from what might be a large hook, and as Matthew watched, the hook—for that's what it was—slowly descended, the body of Sharon dangling from it. Matthew's heart almost stopped . . . but when Sharon's body reached the ground, he saw that she was still alive, that her terrified eyes were open, but that she was tightly bound in the same kind of fishing line that had been strung around Mr. Smudge's neck. He moved towards her.

"Stop," said Savio, raising his hand. "I offered you the chance to see Sharon, but that's all I offered. You can look, Matthew, but you can't touch. No, you're here to offer me some final entertainment."

"And what might that be?" asked Matthew, looking Savio full in the face. Oddly, he felt very little fear; he was, instead, animated by a desire to see Sharon free and safe at any cost. The prospect of his own death troubled him not at all.

"You're going to have a cage fight with my friends here," said Savio, indicating Dick and Harry. "They've been itching to have another shot at you, and I promised them I'd provide it. And there's no escaping this time, Matthew." The two goons made their way towards the cage. Dick opened the door and climbed in. Harry followed him. They turned to face Matthew, looking at him with a species of blood-lust that in previous years he might have found chilling.

"Why not just do the job yourself?" asked Matthew. "I'm sure that would give you great satisfaction."

"It would," said Savio, "but that satisfaction is denied me. Even the greatest of us have to operate within rules, Matthew. I cannot kill you with my own hands, pleasant though that would be, but I can do so through my servants. It's a very acceptable second-best—particularly when the death is slow and painful. As yours will be."

"All right," said Matthew. "But if I'm to die, release Sharon. She hasn't offended you as I clearly must have. Let her go, and have your way with me. I'll put on a magnificent show."

"Oh, no," said Savio. "No, it doesn't work that way. I'm *so* sorry if you felt you could somehow negotiate her release. *Such* a sad misunderstanding."

"Then what do you think will encourage me to climb into the cage with your minions?" asked Matthew. "If you want a show, you need to give me some incentive to participate."

"Do you see the fishing line that's wrapped around your girl?" asked Savio. "You'll see that there's a loop around her neck. One small gesture from me, and that loop will tighten. It's a miserable way to die. No, I think that if you were to give her a vote, Matthew, she would opt for the sort of servitude I offer her—the same yoke that was, for a time, around Hannah Hutchinson's pretty neck. If you don't want to see her die horribly, *get in the cage*." His voice descended an octave on the final sentence.

At that instant, a door at the far end of the hall opened, and Matthew was aware of a foul scent. The giant from the cathedral entered. He stood staring at Matthew for a moment, then lumbered toward him. *So this is it*, Matthew thought. *This is how it ends*. There had been a chance, however slim, that he could take on the Dick and Harry combination, but he knew he could not prevail against the giant as well. He glanced at Savio, expecting to see exultation on his face. To his surprise, he did not.

The door through which he had himself entered opened behind him. Matthew turned, expecting to see yet another malevolent actor—for all he knew the hill was lousy with them. But—"Baron!" he said, the word a joyful exclamation.

"Fearful symmetry, my friend," said Baron. "Fearful symmetry." He moved forward, until he was the same distance from Matthew on one side as the giant was on the other. And there both stayed.

Matthew looked again at Savio. There was, for the first time, something mildly subdued about him. It wasn't that he seemed fearful: *sulky* was perhaps the better word. "Get into the cage," he said to Matthew—and in that instant Matthew realized that he *might* have a chance, however slim. He would not inevitably die that evening. If he could successfully fight off both the broad-shouldered man and the East Asian teen, he might yet leave with Sharon safely in his custody. It was a long-shot, but he had a shot.

"Matthew," said Baron quietly, "I cannot fight at your side, but I can remind you of something. Did you, while in England, receive a gift? There are things I cannot see, but I think you may have spoken with someone whose powers are older than mine."

"Get in the cage!" Savio shrieked—and, even more disturbingly, the giant howled, the guttural note shaking the very floor with its strength.

Of course, thought Matthew, *the vial of water*—the water he'd rubbed on his hands, along with the water from the baptismal font in Salisbury Cathedral. He glanced down at his hands, and he saw, to his astonishment, that they were surrounded by a sheen, a radiant luster. He straightened his back, and moved towards the cage.

Chapter Forty-Five

However his hands might look to himself, they clearly did not look any different to his nemeses. Matthew stepped into the cage and faced them, and Savio clanged the door shut. As Matthew eyed Dick and Harry, they moved slowly, one shifting to the left, the other to the right, with the clear intention of coming at him from two sides. As they shifted, moreover, they drew knives, their own shivs, from their back pockets. Matthew drew his also, but as soon as he removed it, Savio lifted his left hand—and Matthew's knife was ripped away: it shot through the bars and into Savio's grasp. Savio laughed. "I decide who gets weapons," he said. Matthew hoped that Baron might say or do something, but he did not. Which meant, surely, that he could not.

Dick and Harry were now where they wanted to be—level with one another, and in a straight line with Matthew. They both bobbed up and down, one edging forward a step, then the other, each move calculated to force Matthew into attacking one of them, thus leaving his back open to a knife from behind. The hall was silent, except for the sound of the three men breathing.

Harry cried out and took two steps forward, forcing Matthew to face him, his fists clenched and facing upward, karate-style, at his hips; as soon as Matthew turned in this way, Dick darted in and slashed his knife across his back: Matthew felt the metal pass through skin and muscle and whipped around to face the teen, at the same time backing toward the side of the cage. He leaned his now bleeding back against the bars, aware that he was losing blood, and that each passing moment would leave him weaker.

But as he leaned back, and as his two leering adversaries again stood next to each other, menacing him from a distance just a little greater than a lunge would take him, he thought about what the mingled waters of Ynys Enlli and Salisbury Cathedral might have given him—apart from a sheen on his hands. *What's the significance of water?* he asked himself. *Why the fuss?*

Harry darted towards him and thrust at his gut: Matthew jerked himself out of the way just in time to avoid the blade. Dick laughed. "You hurting, Matty?" he sang out. "You hurting bad?"

Water, Matthew thought. *Cleansing, healing, baptism. What good is any of that to me now?* Dick took a run at him, repeating the same move the larger thug had made the moment before. Matthew was fractionally slower this time. It was a closer miss. "Just a matter of time, Matty," said the teen, taunting him.

Matthew was suddenly seized by the impulse to raise his hands—though not as a declaration of surrender—and he directed his palms towards the men menacing him with their knives. "No use trying to surrender—" Savio began, but a shimmering beam of light shot out of each of Matthew's hands, knocking Harry and Dick off their feet and against the far side of the cage, their knives flying through the bars. The force, though brief, was extraordinarily powerful. Its transmission left Matthew feeling strangely energized, as though the light had cleansed his own body of toxins, fatigue, and pain. He straightened his back, stood upright.

"No," Savio moaned. He took a couple of steps back from the cage. "No!"

"What the—!" said Dick, rubbing the back of his head. Harry said nothing. The two men got slowly to their feet, looked at Matthew, looked at Savio, then stumbled to the cage door. Dick opened it, and they both exited, falling over themselves. Outside the cage they made a stumbling run across the cave floor and toward the door.

The giant threw back his head and howled. It was a chilling sound, but it was not triumphant. It was the noise a predator might make at the escape of its prey.

Savio took a step towards Matthew. "Don't imagine you have triumphed, Matthew," he hissed. "I recruit servants by the truckload. I beckon, and they come. You have days left to you. There's a sword dangling over your head."

Matthew was about to respond, but the giant got in first. "No," he growled, his voice harsh, guttural, dark-as-death. "You have had your chance. Our Master is displeased. You must answer to him!" He raised both his hands, and Savio was seized by a force that caught him up and propelled him at the other door—the door leading, for all Matthew knew, to the depths of hell itself.

The giant turned his attention to Matthew, stared at him, howled once more—seeming to double in size as he did so—then wheeled around and lumbered across the floor after Savio. When he passed through the door, it slammed behind him.

Baron's voice came quietly from behind. "Well done. Well done, Matthew."

CHAPTER FORTY-SIX

After Matthew had released Sharon from her bonds; after Matthew and Baron, carrying her, had made their way back along the corridor; after they'd gone to the hospital, and Sharon and Matthew were examined and treated; they'd driven back, the three of them, to Toronto in a rental car, taking Sharon to her apartment and settling her there. Sometime later that day, Matthew asked Baron what he had encountered.

"There is something in the universe we desperately wish were not here," Baron replied. "I'm talking about active evil, conscious malevolence. We can wrap our minds around accidents—an icy road, a marble on the stair, an uncovered well, a frayed wire. These are natural evils—horrible enough in their consequences, but not *willed*." He reached into the air, and plucked out a lit match—then dropped it in the glass of water at his elbow in the restaurant where they were having dinner. "But then," he went on, "there is another category of acts—the rape of children, torture, the murder of innocents. These have a progenitor, an author, a source. You encountered the source." He reached again into the air, and seemed to pull out a handful of fire. It raged in his hand for a moment, then Baron formed a fist, extinguishing it—or not quite, not immediately, for the flames flickered between his fingers a moment longer.

"Sir," said their waitress, hurrying towards them, "I'm sorry, but we don't allow smoking in here."

"Of course not," said Baron, opening both his hands and showing they were empty. "It's a foul habit." He smiled.

"Oh, I'm sorry," she said. "My mistake. I thought you—"

"I was just showing my friend a little magic trick," said Baron. "But I promise there will be no more, Molly." He raised his glass to her, the glass in which he'd dropped the match but which was now conspicuously matchless: "Could I trouble you for some more water? When you have a moment?"

"Of course," she said, and went away to fetch it.

"Now, what can you tell me?" said Baron, returning his attention to Matthew.

"I honestly have no idea," said Matthew. "The light just . . . radiated from my hands."

"Well, I have some idea," said Baron. "I have my own mandate, my own sphere of influence, but as I think you may have intuited, there are others, too. There are more things in heaven and earth, Matthew . . . Who am I misquoting?"

"Hamlet," said Matthew. "I may be a community college boy, but even I know that one."

"Every place has its guardians," said Baron. "Here, in Toronto, there are people like Clara."

"And *you*, it seems," said Matthew.

"And you, too," said Baron, leaning across the table. "We are God's hands, Matthew. I speak metaphorically, of course."

"The ones I met in England were an old gentleman with piercing, bright blue eyes," said Matthew, "and a young gypsy woman who said she was old."

Baron smiled, nodded. "I suspect their names will occur to you later," he said.

★ ★ ★

Matthew checked in with Sharon by phone. "How are you?" he asked.

"I'm fine," she said. "My sister dropped by and she's going to spend the night here. We're just drinking some wine and beginning to think about dinner."

Matthew hesitated a moment. "Are you sure you're fine, Sharon?" he said. "You'd have every reason to feel traumatized. I want you to take as much time off as you need."

Sharon laughed: "Why on earth would I feel traumatized, Matthew?" she said. "It was just a little business trip. It may be the wine, but the details are already getting a bit hazy."

Is she joking? Matthew wondered. *Is she in the grip of post-trau-matic shock? Or is this some merciful intervention—a gift from Clara, or, perhaps, Baron?* "Well, if you change your mind, just send me a text or give me a call," he said.

"You're a kind man," said Sharon. "You know that? I've been telling my sister about you, and she can't believe I work for such a gentleman." She paused a moment, and then: "I think the wine is making me sentimental, Matthew, so I'm going to hang up now. Good night."

"Good night, Sharon," Matthew said.

He sat and thought for a few minutes, then called up his psy-chologist friend, Jordan Barker, and left a message proposing lunch the next day. He hoped he would have time. *A man needs friends*, he thought.

★ ★ ★

That night, after a hot shower, he went to bed early. His back hurt. The emergency room doctor at the hospital had treat-ed his wound, given him antibiotics, and told him to see his own doctor in Toronto the next day. He'd asked a lot of questions, too, but Baron had said something to him quietly, touched his shoulder, and he'd got a glazed look on his face as if he'd just drawn a blank in answer to a tough question. He'd then left to attend to another patient. "Better not to involve the police," Baron had said to Matthew.

Memory was a fragile thing, Matthew realized.

★ ★ ★

He fell asleep quickly, and came back to consciousness in the land he'd visited several times before. It was morning, and he was walking in a garden. The garden was not well-ordered and had areas of wildness, but there were patches of cultivation—white flowers here, red there, olive trees. Matthew walked on, ascend-ing a slight slope. Suddenly, running down the hill towards him, he saw a young woman, modestly dressed. While she was indeed running, which might suggest distress, the look on her face was one of wonder, as though she had seen something that filled her with joy. Matthew pressed on, paying attention, as he walked, to the songs of unfamiliar birds, to unfamiliar scents, to the very different quality of light.

He came to a rock face, and in that rock face were a number of caves, some with large boulders sealing their entrances, some open to the world. His attention was drawn to one in particular, which had a boulder next to the entrance, as though it had not yet been closed, or as though it had recently been rolled back. He walked towards it, hesitated, peered inside.

There, standing in the middle of the small cave, was a woman he recognized. "Clara!" he said.

She smiled at him, raised her hand. "Matthew," she said. "He's gone. He is not here." Matthew woke up, gazed at the ceiling. He felt a great sense of peace. The rest of the night was dreamless.

★ ★ ★

The next morning Matthew opened his eyes to find the sun already shining through his bedroom window. It was going to be hot and humid, he realized, but for now it was comfortable, however much his back might hurt. He rose, showered, shaved, had breakfast and called his doctor's office. He took the elevator downstairs, strode through the lobby, greeted the concierge warmly, passed through the glass doors and out into the sunshine. Instead of going directly to the subway, a short block away, he turned right and walked to High Park. There were joggers on the paths, mothers with children, civil servants and business folk on their way to work. The grass was soft, the trees were green and healthy, and some were in flower. A young man was throwing a frisbee for his dog.

Matthew stopped, breathed deeply. He was alive. His life was charged with meaning. He had good work to do.

Acknowledgments

I am very grateful to the people who read all or part of *The Rogue Wave* at some point, and offered commentary or encouragement. They include Tim Ward, Jane Beharriell, Peter Gould, Penny Irwin, Nathalie Paulin, Rachael Mason, Nina Mason, Muriel Mason, Baron Marcus, Tom Woolsey and Hana Holubec. I am also very grateful to my editor, Kimmy Beach—a splendid writer herself!—and to Chris Needham of Now Or Never.